WHAT A LIFE!
Selected short stories

J. B. Priestley

TURNPIKE BOOKS

These short stories were first published in 'Four-in-Hand', Heinemann 1934
This edition published by Turnpike Books 2014

turnpikebooks@gmail.com

ISBN   9780957233638

Cover artwork by: David Hockney, 'J.B. Priestley' 1973
Ink on paper, 17 × 14", © David Hockney

Typeset by RefineCatch Limited, Bungay, Suffolk

Printed and bound in Great Britain

CONTENTS

WHAT A LIFE!

It was one of those hotels that are called "quiet hotels for gentlefolk." Apparently, gentlefolk have a passion for an atmosphere of dinginess and slight decay. This hotel, like many of its kind, had two lounges: one at the front, in which people merely waited for one another and for the telephone, and one at the back, the "Brown Lounge," in which a number of large pieces of furniture and some gigantic steel engravings waited for the Day of Judgment. It has been often suggested that there should be public lethal chambers for those unfortunates who are bent on suicide. This "Brown Lounge" would make an excellent lethal chamber, for, even as it is, once inside it your thoughts turn naturally to the end of this life. Only young and bold spirits could withstand its insidious melancholy. There are two of them in there now.

"What time does the show start?" said the first young man, who was staying at the hotel. He was engaged in manufacturing motor cars in a provincial town and did not often visit London.

"Half-past eight," said the other young man, who lived in London and was uproariously in the publicity business.

"Just a time for a drink, then," said the other, ringing the bell.

After a minute or two a waiter appeared, a vague, oldish chap, the sort of waiter you expect to find in that sort of hotel.

"Two whiskies," said the first young man.

"Two whiskies, sir," the waiter replied, in a colourless voice. "Yes, sir." And drifted away.

The second young man yawned and then glanced round the room. "What the devil made you come here?" he demanded. "It's a ghastly hole."

"Pretty dismal, I admit. Fellow at the works, one of our designers, said he'd stayed here and it was all right, fairly cheap, and quiet at night. It is quiet, too."

"Quiet! It's dead and buried. Still, I suppose you're out most of the time."

"Gosh, yes. If I wasn't I'd try something livelier than this," the visitor replied, as the waiter returned with the drinks. "Thanks. How much? Here you are, and keep the change."

"Thank you, sir," said the waiter.

"Very quiet here, waiter."

"Very quiet just now, sir." And the waiter picked up his tray and departed.

"I suppose that poor devil will spend the rest of the night waiting for somebody to come in here and order a drink."

"He will," said the second young man. "Not exactly a whirl of excitement, eh? What a life!"

"What a life!"

"Well, cheerio!"

"Cheerio! I suppose we'd better push off if we want to see that show."

They swallowed their drinks and pushed off, leaving two little glasses in the wilderness of the lounge, which sank into deepest quiet and melancholy again.

It was some time, however, before the waiter cleared away those two glasses. He was not very busy and he was not, as a rule, neglectful of his duty, but it happened that he had been waiting for the telephone bell to ring for him, and it rang before he returned to the lounge.

"Is it for me?" he inquired, eagerly, and for the fifth time that evening.

The reception clerk, who knew what it was all about, nodded, and regarded him sympathetically. "I'll put it through to the staff-room," she said; and he hurried away.

There was nothing colourless about his voice now, as he answered the call. It was not the voice of a waiter at all, and there was a terrible urgency in it. As he spoke, a faint ring of moisture appeared just below the line of his greying hair.

"Hello, hello! Yes, that's me," he cried. "A daughter, eh? Yes, yes, that's all right. Is she? You're sure about that? Both of them? Did she say anything? Did she? Is that right? Oh, that's fine. Yes, of course. How soon? All right, then, I'll be round at ten in the morning. And thank you very much. Yes, I'm sure she is. Thank you. And tell her how glad I am, don't forget that. Yes, at ten in the morning. Thank you."

After he had put down the receiver, he drew a long breath, waited a moment and wiped his forehead, then went back to the office. "It's all right," he said to the reception clerk. "I've finished."

"What's the news?" that young lady inquired.

"A daughter, and they're both doing fine."

"That's good. What's the baby like?"

"Only a little one—six pounds and a bit," replied the waiter. "But a healthy kid, they say."

"The little ones are nearly always the best. That's what my cousin says, and she does maternity work. Well, you're a grandfather now."

"So I am," said the waiter. "I never thought of that. An hour ago I was just a father, and now I'm a grandfather. That's queer, you know. Say what you like, miss, but that's queer."

"It's a queer world, that's what I always say. Let me see, haven't I met your daughter? Hasn't she been round here to see you once or twice? Isn't that the one?"

"That's the one," said the waiter, and there was a distinct note of pride in his voice. It suggested that the baby had been lucky to find such a mother, that he had been lucky to have such a daughter, and that even the reception clerk had been lucky in merely meeting such a girl. A proud grandfather, a partly relieved though still anxious father, the waiter now withdrew, to think things over. It had been his job to see his daughter through this queer and difficult time. It was her first baby, and her husband, a good lad but not quite as steady as he might be, was now trying his hand at being a steward on a big cargo boat, and at this moment was somewhere off Sydney. If you had seen the waiter clearing away those two glasses in the Brown Lounge, you would not have realised that his forehead was still damp with perspiration and that his head was humming with plans.

Nothing happened in the Brown Lounge until a little after nine. Then the massive sideboard, the grim armchairs, and the sad steel engravings were disturbed by the entrance of a woman in a rather dubious fur coat. She still carried with her, at once defiantly and anxiously, the red and bronze remains of somewhat hard good looks. She belonged to that mysterious class of women who are often found behaving "like perfect ladies" in places that perfect ladies usually contrive to avoid. Once inside the lounge, this woman rang the bell and then made several movements that suggested, with truth, that she was in an agitated state of mind.

The bell was answered by our friend the waiter. He came in as a waiter, but the moment he saw who it was that had rung the bell, all the waiterishness departed from him and he looked what he was—namely, a surprised and annoyed middle-aged man.

"What do *you* want?" he asked.

"Wanted to talk to you, Joe," the woman replied, promptly, "and I thought the easiest way would be to come in here and not go asking for you at the back. Nobody'll come in, will they?"

"They might."

"Yes, and then they might not," she retorted, with a quick, contemptuous glance round.

"Well?"

"Listen, Joe," she said, in a very, different tone of voice; "what about Alice? How's she getting on? Any news?"

"Who told you about Alice?" he demanded.

"What's it matter who told me? If you want to know, I saw Mrs. Brewer, and she told me you'd told her Alice was going to have a baby. Joe, tell me—what's happened? Is it all right?"

The waiter was silent for a moment.

The woman gave a little yelp of impatience, then seized his arm and shook it. "Come on. Don't stand there like that. What is it? My God if she's——"

"She's all right, at least so far she is," he told her, curtly. "It happened to-night and she's doing well. They telephoned."

"What is it?"

"A girl."

"A girl!" the woman cried, with a little emotional gulp. "A girl! Poor little devil! And they're both all right?"

"They're both all right."

The woman laughed, not very pleasantly. "And now I'm a grandmother. My God!—think of that. Grannie! That puts the years on you, doesn't it? But never mind about that. Listen, Joe—and I'm serious now—I've got to see her. Where is she?"

"Don't you worry. She's all right."

"Don't be a fool, Joe. I've got to see her now. Where is she?"

"I've told you—she's all right. I'm looking after her."

"Do you mean you're not going to let me see her now?" The woman's voice rose almost to a scream.

"Not so much noise," he told her.

"What do I care how much noise I make! You've got to tell me where Alice is and I've got to see her. What do you think I'm made of? I'm her mother, aren't I?"

"You ought to have thought about that a long time ago, before you decided to let some of the flash fellows keep you." The waiter was very grim now. He kept his eyes fixed on those of the woman standing in front of him. They were hard blue eyes that he saw there; and he knew them only too well, especially in this mood of rising anger, heading towards either tears or screams and curses; and as he stared at them, it occurred to him that it was very odd that they should be the eyes of a woman whose name was still his, who was still his wife. They had made no attempt to live together for the last ten years, but they had not been divorced. He did not want to marry again, and she did not seem to find it difficult to call herself Mrs. This and then Mrs. That.

"You always was a mean devil, Joe," his wife proclaimed, and would have enlarged on the topic if he had not interrupted her.

"Yes," he put in, hastily, bitterly, "I've no doubt you've found 'em not so mean where you've been since."

"Well, if you want to know, I have. Now, look here, Joe. I'm the girl's mother, and this is the time when a girl wants to see her mother, and I'm going to see her. Where is she?"

"I'm not going to tell you, and you're not going to see her. Leave her alone. She doesn't want you, and I don't—I only want you to be a long way off."

"Don't worry, I'm not after *you*. You never was any catch at any time, and you're not one now, I can tell you. But I've a right to see my own child. She's my daughter."

"Not now, she isn't," the waiter told her. "You've done. I'll see to that."

"You'll see to a lot, won't you?" she jeered. "One thing's certain though. She's my daughter. She might be yours, and then she might not."

"What!" He shot out a hand, and it fastened on her wrist. "What you trying to tell me now? What's the idea?" He was really ferocious now, quite absurdly unlike any respectable waiter.

This sudden ferocity left the woman uneasy. She wrenched her arm away, and then said, hastily: "Oh, don't be a fool, Joe. You know very well she was yours all right. Where is she? I only want to see her and the baby together. What's the harm in that?"

"That's my business. I've not interfered with you, so don't you interfere with me. You've gone your own way, so just keep to it. And leave Alice alone. I warn you—leave her alone."

At this moment, while they were still glaring at one another, somebody came quietly into the room. She was a tiny old woman, all rings and brooches and lilac silk and black satin, and the waiter knew her well, for she came up from the country regularly to stay at the hotel.

"There you are, waiter," she said, nodding and smiling at him. "Now I needn't ring, need I? Could you get me a nice cup of tea, just a cup?"

"Cup of tea? Certainly, m'," said the waiter, and, without another glance at his wife, he walked out. When he came back, five minutes later, his wife had disappeared.

"You know, waiter," the old lady remarked as he set the tea before her, "some people say tea at night keeps you awake, but I don't find it so. I don't like to go to bed without my cup of tea."

"All a matter of habit, m'," the waiter replied.

"I expect it is," said the old lady.

"I'm sure it is. I like a cup myself."

The old lady, who was a friendly soul, nodded brightly at this, and kept him there a minute or two longer while she told him how long she had been having her late cup and what various relations thought about it. And when she had done, she gave him a sixpenny tip, which was very handsome for a single cup of tea. The waiter could not help reflecting how surprised she would have been if she had learned that the woman who had just gone out was the waiter's wife and a good many other things besides.

Twenty minutes later the bell in the lounge rang again, and the waiter found that the old lady, now sitting in a dream over her empty cup, had company in the shape of a bulky, florid-faced fellow who was smoking a cigar. He looked at the waiter and gave him a tiny knowing grin. The waiter stared for a moment, then promptly relapsed into blank waiterdom.

"Yes, sir?"

"Oh—yes—er—let me see, waiter. I think I'll have a double Scotch and a small soda. I'm not staying here, but that's all right, isn't it? I want to see somebody here." He put a curious emphasis into this last statement.

"That's all right," the waiter muttered, removing the old lady's cup and sugar basin.

"What time is it?" the old lady inquired.

Before the waiter could reply, the newcomer, with a flourish, had taken out a heavy gold watch, and replied: "Five minutes to ten."

"Thank you. Time for me to go to bed, then," she told them both; and the waiter held the door open for her and then retired to get the whisky.

"Two and tenpence," said the waiter, the moment after he had placed the drink in front of the visitor.

The bulky, florid-faced man grinned, and then, with a careful and rather praiseworthy attempt at complete nonchalance, remarked: "You're not going to stand me this one, then Joe?"

"I'm not."

The other handed over three shillings. "Keep the change," he cried, giving a creditable burlesque of a generous visitor.

The waiter said nothing, but merely swept the coins into his pocket and began moving away.

"Wait a minute, Joe, wait a minute. It's no use pretending not to know me."

"Oh, I knew you all right, Dobby," said the waiter, as he stopped and turned. "But what of it?"

"I told you just now I came in here to see somebody. Well, you're him, Joe, you're him."

"How did you know I was here?" the waiter asked.

"I ran into Maggie not half a mile away," the bulky man explained, with a flowing gesture, "and she told me she'd just been having a little talk with you in here. Full of it, she was. You ought to have heard her, Joe. It's a long time since I met Maggie—I mean before to-night—but she's not changed a bit. Still got a lively tongue in her head. Cor!—you ought to have heard her going on about you, Joe. I tell you what it is—you can't handle women, Joe. You never could."

"You didn't come here to tell me that, did you, Dobby?" the waiter inquired. "Because if you did, you're wasting your valuable time." And he made another move as if to go.

"Just a minute, Joe. Don't be so impatient. I came in here to have a look at you, Joe, in your nice waiter's clothes, and I also came in here just to have a look round. Nice quiet hotel, Joe, very nice quiet hotel this. Not the sort of place where anybody would expect any trouble. The police don't worry you much here, Joe, do they? I shouldn't think they would. Very nice and quiet—and gentlemanly. That's what I like about it, Joe—it's gentlemanly."

"Cut it short, Dobby," the waiter told him.

Dobby grinned again. He appeared to be enjoying himself. "Well, Joe, if you want it short, you shall have it short. Now I've got a little scheme. I won't tell you what it is now, but you know my little schemes—you've met 'em before, haven't you, Joe? And for this little scheme I want a nice quiet place to stay in for a week or two, just like this, and so I thought I'd stay here and then you could help me, couldn't you, Joe?"

"Nothing doing," the waiter announced.

"Now don't be hasty, Joe. You don't know what it is you've got to do yet."

"And I don't want to know. But understand this, Dobby—you don't let me in for it and you don't try anything on here."

"Oh, I don't, eh?" The bulky man seemed to be amused.

The waiter was not amused. He was very grim, and there was a curious strained look about his eyes. He came a little nearer now, and though, when he spoke, he was quieter than he had been before, there was a very unpleasant quality in his voice. "You know very well I'm running straight now, Dobby. You're not going to try anything on here, and that's flat."

"Going back on your old friends, eh, Joe? Do you think that's wise?"

"I've told you," said the waiter. "I'm running straight now and I'm keeping straight."

"A nice respectable waiter in a nice respectable hotel. That's the line, is it, Joe?"

Dobby looked at his cigar, put it down, then finished his whisky in one big gulp. He looked up. "It's no good coming the high and mighty with me, Joe, and you know it. How did you get this job? Never mind. I don't want to know. But I'll bet they don't know here that you're an old lag."

The waiter tried to moisten his lips. "They don't," he admitted.

"Of course they don't. Nice respectable, gentlemanly hotel like this. What!—have an old lag as a waiter? Dear me, couldn't be done! A convicted——"

"All right, all right," the waiter interrupted hastily.

"A word from me to the management and where's the nice little waiter's job then?"

"You wouldn't do that, Dobby," the waiter cried.

"I don't want to do it, Joe, but if an old friend won't do a little job for me, quite a safe job, safe as houses, well, then, I might have to make trouble. And that would be very, very easy."

"Why can't you leave me alone? I'm not interfering with you. I've finished with you lot. I've had my medicine—and that's a damn' sight more than you've had yet, Dobby, don't forget that."

"Ah, you see, Joe, I'm not only lucky but I'm clever," Mr. Dobby protested airily. "I don't look it, I know. But I'm clever."

"I'm going straight. I earn what I make, and I'm interfering with nobody. For God's sake, leave me alone, Dobby."

"Can't do that, Joe. Sorry, but it can't be done. You can't go back on your old friends like that. If you help me with this little idea of mine, there's no trouble coming to you, nothing but a little present from an old friend. But if you're going to be awkward, Joe, you're not going to get away with it. We can't have you pretending to be respectable any longer. You're losing this job, see? And you won't get another in a hurry, will you? And then there's this daughter of yours who's just had the baby."

"You've got hold of that, too, have you?" said the waiter, bitterly. "Not much you miss, is there, Dobby?"

"Got it all from Maggie to-night. I tell you, Joe, when women are angry, they spill it all. You don't know how to manage 'em, Joe, and that's where you get yourself into trouble. Now what's it going to be? Are you going to be awkward or am I?"

The waiter came nearer still, very close indeed, leaning on the little table and gradually lowering his head. He looked monstrously unlike any possible waiter; a dangerous man. "Now you've got to listen to me a minute, Dobby," he began, in a tone that was hardly above a whisper. "It's taken me some time to get going. I'm all right here. But if you shop me, I'll have to go."

"Yes, and then—what?"

"I know. You needn't tell me. I'm telling you now. If you shop me, and they turn me off here, I've finished. It's taken me years to get as far as this, but it won't take five minutes to push me back again. I'm through then. But what about you, Dobby, what about you?"

"What d'you mean?" Mr. Dobby must have been feeling rather uneasy, for he was blustering a little now. "You can't shop me, Joe, and you needn't think it. Cleverer men than you have tried to do that, and they missed the bus all right."

The waiter produced what must have been the shortest and most unpleasant laugh ever heard in that room. He put out a hand, resting all his weight on the other, and though it was a waiter's hand, it was very large and powerful. "I shan't bother about that, Dobby," he whispered. "I'll do it all myself. I'll put you where you won't make any trouble again. I shan't have any work to do, and I shan't want any. I'll spend all my time looking for you, Dobby, and when I've found you, I'll make a good job of it."

Mr. Dobby was no longer as florid-looking as he had been before, but he tried to carry off the situation. "And that's been said before, and tried before, and it hasn't come off."

"It will this time," said the waiter. "I shan't do it myself, either. There'll be two of us. I know where Raspy is. Raspy's out, y'know, Dobby."

"Raspy's out," the other admitted, uneasily. "But he's dead."

"He's not dead. I saw him, spoke to him, not two months since, and I know where he is now. He wants to meet you again, Dobby, but he thinks you're a long way off, in South America. You should hear what he says about you, Dobby, and what he'd like to do to you. And the minute I'm turned off here I'm going to Raspy, and then we'll come looking for you, Dobby. And I mean that. Leave me here and I'll interfere with nobody, but get me turned out into the street again and I'm a desperate man, see?"

"I see, Joe."

The waiter drew back from the table. "So just take your little schemes somewhere else, Dobby. You're not trying anything on here."

Mr. Dobby rose from his chair and made for the door. "All right, Joe. Keep on being a good boy. So long." He carried it off with his customary swagger, but there could be no denying the fact that he had lost the rubber.

The waiter did not follow him out. He stood motionless for several minutes, breathing deeply, like a man who had just saved his skin only by the fraction of an inch. Then something seemed to happen to him; he shrank a little; the light died out of his eyes; certain lines vanished from his face; and, in fact, he turned into a middle-aged waiter again. There were a glass and an empty soda-water bottle to remove. He removed them.

"Well, here we are again," said the first young man.

"I'll push off in a minute, old man," said the second young man, seating himself on the arm of a chair. "I've a busy day to-morrow."

"You've time for a quick one, anyhow."

And he rang the bell. The same old waiter appeared. "Two whiskies, please."

"Two whiskies, sir," the waiter replied, in a colourless voice. "Yes, sir." And drifted away.

The second young man yawned and then glanced round the room. "Don't stay in this hole again."

"Wait a minute," cried the first young man. "This room has actually had a customer or guest or visitor in it since we left. I smell cigar smoke and I see here the stump of a cigar. You know my methods, Watson."

"I can't believe it. I think the waiter must have come in and smoked it on the sly."

The waiter returned. "I'm going off duty now, sir, but if you want anything else, the night porter'll get it for you."

"Thanks, but I shan't. Here you are."

"Thank you, sir."

"Still very quiet here, waiter."

"Very quiet just now, sir." And the waiter picked up his tray and departed.

"Not a bad chap, that waiter, but—my hat!—what a life!"

"What a life! Well—cheerio!"

"Cheerio!"

GOING UP?

Milly stared, hesitated a moment, and then let her hand slide away from her companion's arm. There was nothing to be seen but the Underground Station Exit, a few late passengers, and a young man in a blue uniform waiting there to collect tickets. But then this particular blue uniform belonged to Mr. James Underwood. What Jimmy was doing on duty at this time, taking tickets, Milly could not imagine, but there he was. For one second, she felt a little frightened. Then she decided that it would serve him right, do him good, just teach him a thing or two. A girl couldn't stop in, all night and every night, just because Jimmy Underwood had lost his temper and turned sulky. As a matter of fact, she had stayed in several nights, waiting for him to come round and say he was sorry, and had been so fidgety and cross that her mother, who was always saying that girls these days didn't know what a home was, the way they went out night after night, told her very plainly she liked a bit of peace in the evening. "And if you can't settle, Miss, take yourself out and leave it to them that can."

But then Milly's mother did not know she had had words with Jimmy Underwood, after going out with him months and months. Milly was an independent girl. She kept things to herself. Nearly all the girls at Borridges' ("You Can Buy It At Borridges'!") were like that, not stand-offish, not conceited, but just independent. If you have been to Borridges', you have probably seen Milly. Every weekday, from nine to six, she wears a chocolate-and-gold uniform, as pretty as anything in a musical comedy, and lives in a little cage that perpetually travels from the basement to the roof garden. "Gowing up?" she inquires, rather disdainfully, as if all the best people ought to be going down. But if you try going down, you find she is still disdainful. They are like that, too, these girls at Borridges', and Milly happens to be one of the best-looking of the dozen or so in chocolate-and-gold, though her nose gives her some anxiety, being one of those noses that insist upon going up and never coming down. If Jimmy had first seen her at Borridges', he would probably never have dared to suggest that she might accompany him to the pictures, but, as it happened, he had made her acquaintance in the High Street of the suburb in which they both ate and slept.

Seeing Jimmy taking tickets there, Milly, after hesitating a moment, made up her mind he was to be "shown." She grabbed her companion's arm again, looked up at him sweetly, talked very rapidly, and then, when they were within a yard or two of Jimmy, laughed very heartily at nothing. Unfortunately, her companion, a tall young man from the music department at Borridges', merely looked startled and began fumbling for the tickets. Milly reminded herself, however, that he was in evening dress, and in this light his resemblance to John Gilbert and several other film stars was more marked than usual.

Jimmy did not look as crushed as he ought to have done, but his usual broad grin was absent. He gave her a nod, and then looked elsewhere, humming loudly. But there was time for him to catch her brief condescending smile. Once past the barrier, she took her companion's arm again, looked up at him, and laughed, her face very close to his shoulder. At the entrance, they stood for a moment, and Milly glanced back. Yes, Jimmy was watching her.

But it was necessary, before she reached home, to put the young man from the music department in his place. It was all right going once in a while to the Palais de Danse with him; but if he thought now he could try any John Gilbert stuff with her, he was mistaken. The sudden intimacy of the Underground Station vanished, and it was a very bewildered and subdued young man, not at all like John Gilbert, who said Good-night to Milly just outside her door.

"And that," she said later, concluding her account of the matter to her sister Dot, "will do Jimmy Underwood a bit of good, if you ask me." There is a limit to independence. Somebody has to be told what is happening to us, and in Milly's case, that somebody was Dot, who shared the same small bedroom and indeed the same small bed.

"What's he like?" asked Dot.

"Jimmy? You know what Jimmy's like—"

"No, not Jimmy," cried Dot, who had heard all about Jimmy months ago. "The other one, the one you've been out with."

"Oh, him! He's all right, for what he is. A bit soft and sloppy." Milly inspected a stocking and had clearly dismissed the young man from the music department from her mind. "You just wait now. You'll see Jimmy coming round, so sorry for himself it'll nearly choke him."

About the middle of the morning, three days later, days during which Mr. James Underwood had given no sign of his existence, Milly shot her lift up from the basement to the ground floor. "Gowing up?" she enquired.

"That's right," said a voice. Jimmy Underwood, no longer in uniform but very neat in a blue suit and a gentlemanly cap, slipped into the lift. He sat down, gave her a quick grin, then looked at her very severely.

"Look 'ere, Milly, what's the idea?" he began.

The bell began too. Having recovered from her first shock of surprise, Milly, with great presence of mind, sent the lift down and then immediately stopped it, so that the two of them were suspended between the ground floor and the basement. Apparently, the bell resented this arrangement.

This visit, in Milly's eyes, represented capitulation. Jimmy would not have ventured into the brilliant jungle of Borridges' unless he had wanted to see her very badly. She felt she was mistress of the situation. Jimmy was not going to get off easily. He was too cocky, with his, "That's right," and his, "What's the idea?"

"And what you doin' here, Jimmy Underwood? And how d'you mean—'what's the idea'?" She looked at him haughtily, very trim, almost severe, in her chocolate-and-gold uniform.

"Well, what I want to know's this," Jimmy began again.

But the bell was really angry. It could no longer be ignored.

"Blast you!" Milly muttered, and shot them both up to the second floor. Once there she instantly became the faintly disdainful and very efficient creature we all know. "Gowing up?"

A Purple Hat wanted the Hardware, and an Imitation Sable wanted the Coats (as well she might), and Milly hastily deposited the pair of them on the fourth and fifth floors respectively. She then took herself and Jimmy to the sixth and final floor.

"Who was that feller?" Jimmy went on.

Milly raised her eyebrows. "A friend of mine. Any objection?"

"Oh no, not-at-all, not-at-all," cried Jimmy, trying to put so many different meanings into his tone that he merely sounded idiotic. And this, of course, annoyed him. "If you want to spend yer time with imitation West-End sheeks, just get on with it, that's what I say, just get on with it!"

But what Milly did get on with, just then, was her business as director of the flying cage, for at that moment she caught sight of a black coat. Mr. Murdson, the assistant-manager. She descended so suddenly, so quickly that Jimmy gasped. She was pulled up at the third floor. "Gowing daown?" she enquired, very coldly.

The little clergyman standing there looked at her wistfully over the top of his large and ridiculously-shaped parcel, "No, up," he said faintly, and had the gate slammed in his face.

"Y'know, Milly," said Jimmy, standing up now to make himself heard, "I been meanin' to come round only I couldn't."

"Oh? Pity, isn't it?" It is very difficult to be cutting when you have to shout and your back is turned to your hearer, but Milly did what she could.

"It's like this." But then the bell began again, and all she heard was something about Tuesday and nights, from which she gathered that he had been suddenly put on late duty. This was excuse enough, but she was not ready to forgive him yet. He was still too cocky by half and seemed to think he owned her. Meanwhile, however, the bell seemed to think it owned them both.

They stopped at the ground floor, where quite a lot of idiotic people were waiting. They still waited when she opened the door and said, "Going up?" They were waiting for Jimmy to get out. But Jimmy was not getting out. Embarrassed, brick-red, he flattened himself against the back wall of the lift, taking up as little space as he could. The others poured in and Milly began to distribute them among the various floors. Every time there was a moment's silence, she could hear Jimmy's heavy breathing. He was getting tired of this. And serve him right too.

A fattish woman with a hook nose announced that she had changed her mind and would return to the ground floor. This was too much for Jimmy, who was nearly bursting with explanations. He could wait no longer.

"I was coming round on Sunday any'ow," he cried, as they descended.

"I beg your pardon," said the fattish woman, staring at him.

"I was talkin' to the young lady," Jimmy muttered.

Milly felt herself going red all round the back of her neck. Deeply mortified, she kept her eyes fixed on the lift shaft. Just like Jimmy to go and make her look silly like that! And then what if this woman went and complained? She looked the complaining and reporting sort. It was Milly's experience that the fattish ones with the hooked noses were the worst. However, the woman never said anything, and Milly watched her waddling away on the ground floor, towards the entrance, with a feeling of relief. Nobody was waiting, so she dropped into the basement, which was quiet that morning.

Then she turned on Jimmy, who was still looking uncomfortable. What did he want to go and say that for? Was he trying to get her into trouble or what?

"All ri'. Sorry," muttered Jimmy, who being a public person himself, when on duty, knew that he had been at fault. "I was only goin' to say I was coming round any'ow Sunday, but when I sees you with that feller and after what you'd said—"

"And what had I said?" cried Milly, with sudden fierceness.

"You know what you said all right," retorted Jimmy, who was a bold man but shrank from repeating lovers' vows in Borridges' basement. Then he looked at her, and his expression changed. "Never seen yer in the old uniform before, Milly. Suits yer no end. Posh, eh?"

"Not so bad." She tried to sound very distant, but it was hard with Jimmy looking at her like that. The bell rang. Let it ring. They could wait a minute. Poor old Jimmy. After all, it took a bit of doing, coming here and trying to make it up in the lift.

"Specially the 'at," Jimmy went on, encouraged now.

But this was where he went badly wrong. The uniform *was* all right, but the fancy chocolate-and-gold cap, like a chef's in shape and like nothing else on earth in general effect, was the one thing about it that Milly hated. And at that moment the bell rang again, insistently, as if to remind her that she was there to wear a silly cap and take silly people up and down and let them poke corners of their silly parcels into her eye.

"Oh, don't talk so soft!" She sent the lift moving up.

"Well, what's the matter now?" Jimmy was aggrieved.

"Gowing up?" No, they wanted to go down. She shut the door in their faces with a bang. Off they went again, past the first floor, up and up.

"Eh?" Jimmy was as insistent as the bell. "What 'ave I said this time?"

"Oh, shut up! Don't bother me." She stopped at the third floor. "Gowing up?"

Yes, they were, all three ladies, and two of them pointed out that they had been waiting there several minutes, stared curiously at the glowering Jimmy, and told one another that really upon their word, the service at Borridges' was not what it was, not at all what it was. They were making for the tea-room.

"And I hope it chokes you," Milly told herself, as she let them out. Jimmy was muttering something again, but after giving him one angry look, she put her chin in the air and turned away. Before she could close the door of the lift, an elderly lady came round the corner and there, bending at her elbow, was the young man from the music department.

"This lift, madam," he was saying, "will take you to the ground floor, near the entrance." He was at his best, the young man from the music department, in situations of this kind, quite the gentleman. He handed the elderly lady over to the care of Milly, and John Gilbert himself could not have done it better. He gave Milly a bright smile, and Milly gave him back a smile even brighter and turned half round so that Jimmy should see a bit of it. She was sure that Jimmy would recognise him. She could feel Jimmy recognising him, stiffening all over.

On the ground floor, Jimmy stepped out of the lift after the elderly lady, then turned and faced Milly, looking at her meaningly.

"What about it then, Milly?" he began, evidently a bit sorry for himself now.

"Gowing up?" said Milly to the two girls who came up. They wanted the Furnishings. She saw Jimmy standing there, a few feet away now, still watching her face. She saw him purse up his lips to whistle softly, an old trick of his, and then swing round awkwardly, making for the entrance. And then she went soaring out of sight.

She spent the rest of that morning hardening her heart. Outwardly, she was as calm, efficient, and faintly disdainful as ever, a pretty automaton in chocolate-and-gold that spent its days moving vertically in a cage. But her real self was busy all the time telling Jimmy what she thought of him, pointing out exactly why he was not good enough for a girl at Borridges', giving examples of his stupidity, his clumsiness, his lack of taste and tact. These conversations, in which Jimmy's part was merely to make occasional moaning replies, never reached any definite conclusion, and it is rather surprising that she should have taken so much trouble over so contempt-ible a figure. It is also surprising that she should have refused, without any show of reluctance, an invitation from the young man from the music department to visit the Palais again with him.

The following day was one of those long dragging miserable affairs. Borridges' was filled with people who could not make up their minds whether they wanted the basement or the roof garden. Some of them, Milly decided, would not have been satisfied if they had been given the earth. The evening, which Milly spent at home, was so dull that she was positively glad to see her Aunt Flo, who looked in about nine. Aunt Flo could tell fortunes with cards, and once more she told Milly's. As usual there was something about a letter and a journey. The only new and exciting item was not a pleasant one. A fair woman, Aunt Flo said, lowering her voice and goggling her eyes, would soon come into Milly's life and make trouble. Milly must beware. Milly promised that she would beware. Then, after drinking two cups of tea and nibbling at a piece of stale chocolate cake, she did a little indolent ironing and trailed up to bed.

It was not until ten minutes past eleven the next morning that life really began again. And, strangely enough, it began with the arrival in Milly's lift of a certain fair woman. There was no doubt as to her fairness. She was a dazzling blonde, very smart, very dashing, though all, Milly decided at once, in the cheapest and vulgarest style. The sort that girls see through immediately, but also the sort—alas—that seem to take in the men every time. She had a man with her. She would have. And her raspberry-jam lips were smiling at him, this escort of hers.

"Now, Jimmy," she was cooing, "don't you worry, deear. I shan't keep you long in this place."

Yes, it was Jimmy Underwood, and he was wearing a new grey suit and a new grey soft hat, and really he looked so smart, she would not have known him at any distance. She wished with all her heart he had kept at a distance and she had not known him.

"Gowing up?" she said miserably.

The fair woman—some people might have called her a girl, but Milly knew better—raised what was left of her eyebrows and then nodded condescendingly. Jimmy, this new and horrible Jimmy, merely gave her a glance. She might have been anybody.

They went as far as the fifth floor and all the way up they stood very close together, and the woman whispered and laughed softly. She was, we repeat with Milly, that kind of woman. Didn't know how to behave herself in a lift, a public place. Probably didn't know how to behave herself anywhere. And Jimmy was obviously enjoying it. Well, of course, that finished him altogether, she decided somewhere between the third and fourth floors. If he didn't know the difference between a creature like that, all peroxide and lipstick and vamp stuff, and a decent girl, well, of course, there was nothing more to be said.

She watched them depart on the fifth floor, still almost hanging round each other's necks and carrying on in the silliest and most disgusting way. But she found herself compelled to admit that the woman did look smart, even though she might never see thirty again. And Jimmy too looked very neat, quite the gentleman. He had never taken so much trouble with himself all the times he had gone out with her. Just like a man that! He must wait until he had got hold of that retired chorus girl, that barmaid out for the day, that third-rate imitation film vamp, to smarten himself up and buy new clothes.

"Gowing down?" Of course it didn't matter to her. "Fourth Floor. Yes, Gentlemen's Tailoring round to the left. No, the next floor below, Madam, for the Gowns and Evening Wraps." It didn't matter in the least. She had already told Jimmy what she thought about him. "Gowing down?"

But who was she? Where had Jimmy found her? Obviously, they were already very thick, though a woman like that would be thick with any man in no time. "No, Madam, gowing down. Take the next lift for the Toys and Games." Perhaps he had been carrying on with her all the time. The thought made her want to send the lift down to the very bottom with a bang. "Second Floor. Boots and Shoes straight forward. Gowing down?"

The next time she arrived at the fifth floor they were waiting there, and the woman was looking up at Jimmy and rolling her eyes in a manner she no doubt thought very attractive. Unfortunately Jimmy himself seemed to think it very attractive too. He seemed completely gone on her. Milly wanted to shake him, he looked so silly.

"The graound flaw," said the woman very haughtily, looking at Milly as if she were hardly there. There were no other passengers in the lift. Milly caught a fleeting glimpse of Jimmy and thought, for that one moment, he looked rather uncomfortable. But when she contrived to examine his face again, he was smiling down at the creature by his side, who was clinging to his arm and telling him she could not endure the motion of these lifts. Milly did what she could to make that motion all the more unpleasant.

Before they had reached the ground floor, however, the woman changed her mind and announced to Milly that she wished to be taken up to the third.

"You'll have to wait now," said Milly firmly.

The woman gave a loud sniff.

"Gowing down," Milly retorted. And down they went, to the basement, where Milly stayed as long as she dared, with her nose and chin in the air, giving her two passengers no sign that she recognised their existence. She heard them whispering and giggling, however, and so contrived an audible sniff or two herself before she finally landed them on the third floor.

She had not made more than two journeys before she found herself faced with them again. It was a fairly quiet morning, and there was nobody else on that floor.

"Gowing up?" she said, looking steadily at anything but them.

"We've been waiting here three minutes," said the woman severely. "Haven't we, Jimmy deear? Three minutes! Disgraceful, I call it. Take us down to the first floor."

"You want the next lift," said Milly, her face burning. She turned to an elderly gentleman who was strolling past. "Gowing up?"

"All right then," the woman cried. "The Roof Garden." And she marched into the lift and dragged Jimmy after her.

Dizzily swinging between tears and temper now, Milly shut the door. She wanted to kick the elegant panelling. She wanted to stamp and stamp, and then scream. Mechanically, she set the lift on its upward journey to the roof garden. And this was Jimmy, this fellow who, not content with forgetting everything he had told her, must let his brute of a painted blonde come here ordering about and treating her as if she was dirt. It was too much for Milly.

When they arrived at the top, the woman stood there, a figure of outrageous impudence, waiting for Milly to open the lift-door. But Milly did not open it. Nobody was wanting the lift on that floor.

"Well; we're there, aren't we?" cried the woman.

"Yes, you are," Milly replied, trembling with vexation, "and I hope this time you're satisfied. People that don't know their own minds oughter try the stairs for a change—"

"Oh!" The blonde's voice went up and up and her eyebrows went with it. "Oh!"

"Yes, oh!" cried Milly vindictively. She threw open the door and then turned fiercely on Jimmy, now looking rather shamefaced. "And as for you, Jimmy Underwood, I don't know what you think about yourself—"

"What's that got to do with you, miss?" said the blonde sharply. "Never heard of such a thing! I shall report you. Yes, I shall. I shall report you."

Milly was on the point of telling her where to take her reporting, but suddenly she realized what it meant. Borridges' policy was first and last to keep their customers pleased with themselves, and a report would be fatal. The tears welled up, and she bit her lip. "All right," she muttered, "report if you like—"

But at this point, Jimmy intervened or, rather, charged in. " 'Ere, chuck it, Cissie," he said gruffly to the blonde. "I told you you were overdoin' it. It's all right, Milly."

The woman suddenly became a different person. You would not have thought it was the same face. First she gave a short laugh, then she wrinkled her nose at Jimmy, then she presented Milly with a companionable wink. "I leave you to it," she said, and the next moment she was gone.

Jimmy nodded in the direction taken by the blonde. "Our Albert's wife," he explained. "You've 'eard me talk about her. A good sort, but she overdid it. Overdoes everything, she does. It was 'er idea. Not the game. I see that. 'Ere, I'm sorry, Milly. I am, straight. Oh, what the—!"

And before Milly had the slightest chance of telling him once again, and in stronger terms, what she thought about him, Jimmy had swept her back into the lift and given her a hug and a kiss. All in a flash, and not an unpleasant flash either.

"Oo!" cried Milly, a minute or two later. Somebody was standing there. She was flushed, still a little damp, and rather dishevelled.

"Gowing up?" she said, wildly.

He was a humorous, fattish, shabby man, who pulled away at an ancient pipe. (Perhaps he was an author.) He looked at her quizzically, jerked a thumb at the glass roof, shook his head, and said: "Going up? No, not yet."

"Sorry!" Milly giggled. "I meant—gowing down."

And all the way down, the fattish, shabby man made little bad jokes. The other two did not mind at all.

ADVENTURE

It was a fine night, so Hubert climbed the steps of a 13 bus. He was returning from the Tumbersomes, pleasant but dullish people who were friends of the family. They had given him a fairly good dinner and three rubbers of conversational bridge, and they had left him dissatisfied. From the top of his bus, which carried him down the brilliantly-lighted but now almost deserted length of Baker Street, Hubert sighed for adventure. There is something theatrical about these thoroughfares when the hour is approaching midnight and it happens to be fine. They look like stage "sets." They suggest that at any moment the most picturesque drama might begin. Hubert, a reader of fiction, a playgoer, a dropper-in at the livelier film shows, never saw the streets at this hour without hoping that something exciting, mysterious, romantic, would happen to him. But somehow it never did.

In a few minutes, he would leave the bus, walk down one street, turn up another and arrive at the little flat that he shared with his friend, John Langton. And John, who never sighed for adventure, would be sitting there, sucking at a pipe and peering over his spectacles at some mouldy book on Egyptology, and he would look up and say: "Hello, young Hube! How did the dinner go off? And what about a spot of tea?" They would make some tea, yarn and yawn for another half-hour, and then drift off to bed. The evening would be over, finished, completely extinguished, and the next morning he would go to the office and John would go to the Museum. Meanwhile, time was flying. Hubert was twenty-three, which seemed to him to be on the dreadful verge of middle age. True, John was twenty-eight, and though nothing exciting ever happened to him, he did not appear to care, but then if you are interested in Egyptology, you probably hardly know whether you are twenty-eight or a hundred, you would not recognise an adventure if you saw one. Poor John! It must be pretty awful to be like that, Hubert reflected. But then it was rather disappointing when you were not like that, when you were ready for adventures that somehow never appeared. London, Hubert decided, did not live up to its appearance. Nor did he stop to think that a great many people in London were hard at work preventing adventures from reaching him.

He glanced round at the other passengers on the bus. It was difficult to see their faces, but they looked, as usual, a dull lot. No men disfigured by strange scars stared fixedly at him. No beautiful girls raised tear-brimmed eyes to his, mutely appealing for help. Not a Lascar or a Chinaman was in sight. Yet the streets, so brightly illuminated and yet so mysterious, looked as if they were awaiting Haroun al Raschid himself. They were a fraud.

Then his glance was caught by a golden gleam. It came from the coffee-stall at the corner. Hubert's acquaintance with minor fiction and journalism had taught him that there is something adventurous and romantic about coffee-stalls. So far his own experience with them had suggested that it was only the stomach, compelled as it was to entertain slabs of dubious cake and cups of hot treacly liquid, that found adventure there, and not very pleasant adventure either. But, as usual, hope and the romantic imagination triumphed over experience. Hubert left the bus at the corner, and ordered a cup of coffee and a piece of cake that he did not want.

There were only two or three men there, but they had contrived to set going one of those mysterious and unending arguments so delightful to the Cockney in his hours of ease.

"An' I tell yer 'e did," cried one of them.

"Like 'ell 'e did!" the other retorted, with great scorn.

" 'Ere," said the first man, more passionately, " 'ere, did yer read it in the piper or didn't yer? Thet's all I wanner know. Did yer or didn't cher?"

"In the piper! In the piper! Did I read it in the piper!" the other sneered.

"Well, what's the matter wi' that? 'Ere, Charlie," he appealed to the owner of the stall, " 'e can't get away from it, can 'e? I seen it in the piper an' I'll bet you seen it in the piper."

"Dessay I did, chum," replied the man behind the counter, diplomatically, "but can't call to mind everything I sees in the paper."

Hubert deliberately switched off his attention and retreated a few paces from the stall. He did not want to hear any more of this stuff. Better to be back in the flat, talking to old John. He sighed. Apparently the best thing he could do was to resign himself to the fact that the evening was over and to stroll home. As usual, he had drawn blank at the coffee-stall. It was part of the general fraud. He tried the coffee and found it hotter and more treacly than ever. What a life!

But at that moment a taxi came rattling up and stopped dead at the stall, with a little scream. The driver turned round and shouted something to the interior. Immediately, the door was flung open, a man almost fell out of it, and came zigzagging over to the stall. In his haste he cannoned into Hubert, and Hubert's coffee and cake went flying. Paying no attention to this mishap, the newcomer arrived at the counter and implored Charlie, whom he appeared to know quite well, to let him have some cigarettes. Having done that, however, he turned round, looked at Hubert, and burst into speech.

"Sorry, ol' man. Very, very sorry. Couldn't be helped. Y'know, couldn't possibly be helped. Now you have some more. What is it? Give it a name." He was a tallish, stout man, and, like Hubert himself, in evening clothes, but, unlike Hubert, not quite a gentleman. At least, that is what Hubert decided.

"It doesn't matter," Hubert told him. "I—really—I didn't particularly want the stuff."

The other looked at him drolly. "Then why have it, why order it, why pay for it, why hold it in the hand, if you don't want it?"

Hubert laughed, not without embarrassment. "Oh, I just stopped here—on my way home, you know—just—er—for something to do. I mean, I wasn't particularly hungry or thirsty or—er—anything."

"Too early to turn in, eh? Anything better than going home, eh? That's the spirit."

"Well, you know how you feel sometimes," said Hubert.

The other patted him on the shoulder. "I do. I feel like it all the time. Only dead once, aren't we?" he went on, as if he and Hubert had gone into this question and arrived at this momentous discovery together. "Now, I'll tell you what. You come with me, ol' man. I'm just going to a little club, quite private, not a mile from here. You come with me. As my guest, my friend, my companion in distress. I'll show you something."

Hubert hesitated. The man was obviously rather tight, though not so tight as he had first appeared, and a visit to some piffling night club in his company did not sound very attractive. "Well, I don't know——" he began.

"The only thing is," said the man earnestly, coming closer, "can you keep a tongue in your head? That's important. Is mum the word with you? If not, no go. Must withdraw invitation."

This decided Hubert. There was a suggestion here of real adventure, and the least he could do was to accept it. So he thanked the man, and agreed to accompany him.

"That's the way," said the other approvingly, and pointed to the waiting taxi. "In we go, and off we go." He seized Hubert by the arm, shouted to the driver, and in another minute they were driving down Upper Baker Street.

"Boys together," said Hubert's companion, with enthusiasm. "And the Night is Young."

"What is this club?" asked Hubert.

"One moment," said the other. "Let's have names. Any names will do, but must have 'em. Can't carry on a proper conversation without names. Now mine's Lux—L-u-x—just the same as the stuff for washing clothes, the very same—but older, much, much older. What's yours?"

Mechanically, Hubert was on the point of giving his own surname when it struck him that that might not be wise. You never knew what might happen. Besides, if this was an adventure, a false name would help it on a little. So he replied: "Watson."

"Very good," said Mr. Lux, almost as if a great load had been taken off his mind. "Now then, you wanted to know what this club is, didn't you? Well, I'll tell you, though mum is still the word. Don't forget that, Watson ol' man. This club is the Roumanian Sports Club."

"What?"

"The Roumanian Sports," replied Mr. Lux solemnly. "You can divide it in two. We don't get in on the Roumanian side. But we get in on the sports. Watson and Lux—sportsmen. How's that?" He peered out of the window. "Getting nearly there now."

Hubert had no idea where they were. For the last five minutes, the taxi had been winding its way through mysterious side-streets. Nor was he any wiser when it finally stopped and they emerged into a darkish and deserted street. Mr. Lux led the way down a sort of courtyard, and they climbed several flights of creaking stairs. At the top of these stairs and at the end of a corridor was a door with a miniature sheepskin fastened to it. Mr. Lux rubbed a hand up and down this sheepskin, and after a minute or so, the door slowly opened and a head looked out at them.

"Has Gregory gone to Bucharest?" Mr. Lux promptly inquired of this head.

The head wagged, then withdrew. The door was opened a little more, and evidently they were now free to enter. Hubert was thrilled. That strange question about Bucharest was a sort of countersign. This was the real thing.

The club consisted of one room of no great size. At one end was a bar. At the other, a most repulsive-looking negro was hammering away at a piano. In the very small space left open in the centre, a few couples were dancing. The rest of the company was seated at little tables. There may have been some Roumanians there. No doubt the atmosphere was Balkan, for it was excessively thick, smoky and smelly. But most of the people seemed to belong to places much nearer home than Bucharest, and a great many of them looked very tough. If Hubert had wanted some sinister company, now he had got it. And having got it, he did not like the look of it at all. Still, this was certainly an adventure.

Mr. Lux pushed his way to a table near the bar and Hubert followed him. "Shove your hat and coat underneath, Watson, ol' man," he said, "and keep your eye on 'em. Never know when they might be wanted here. And remember," he whispered impressively, "the word is—"

"Mum," replied Hubert, who suddenly felt very daring.

"A-ha, a-ha!" cried the other, looking up. A flat-faced young man, with a hard eye, had arrived at their table. He was followed by two girls, one of them red-haired and slight, rather pretty, the other a metallic blonde, and both of them over-painted and cheaply if showily dressed. They were not the kind of girls Hubert understood at all, outside fiction and the drama, and as for the flat-faced young man, he looked a most unpleasant fellow. But Mr. Lux greeted all three expansively.

"Well, Luxy boy," said the flat-faced one, carelessly, as he sat down, "what's doin'?"

The two girls greeted Mr. Lux, one of them, the blonde, patting his cheek. They sat down on each side of Hubert, very close. He was introduced. The flat-faced young man was Meakin, the red-haired girl Patsy, the blonde, who was now squeezing Hubert's arm, was Dot.

Mr. Lux ordered whiskies all round, and then explained to his friend Meakin what was doing. Apparently it was an explanation that demanded not only a confidential whispering but also a great many strange nods and winks. Meanwhile, the two girls, sipping their whiskies, were making a friend of Hubert. They did this by coming even closer than they were before, squeezing his arms, tapping his feet with theirs, talcing his hand from time to time, and talking about him as if he were not there, as if indeed he had been a nice new toy they had just been given.

"What I say, Patsy, my dear," said the terrible Dot, "is that he's a Nice Boy." And she wriggled forward and put her cheek to his for a moment.

"And I say he's a little gentleman as well," said Patsy, looking at Hubert with narrowed eyes. Then she gave a little laugh. There was something about this laugh that made Hubert feel very uncomfortable. He much preferred Patsy, who was the prettier, probably the more intelligent, and certainly the less brazen, and he could not help feeling that she thought him a fool. He tried a cynical laugh in reply, but as something went wrong with it half-way, he produced what he hoped was regarded as a weary shrug of the shoulders and then sat bolt upright.

"Course he is," cried Dot, leaning heavily against him.

"That's the way, Watson, ol' man," Mr. Lux called across. "You enjoy yourself."

"You leave him alone, Luxy," said Dot, in pretended indignation.

Hubert caught a sardonic gleam from the little eyes of the flat-faced Meakin. He was not sure that he was enjoying himself. He decided to take his leave of the Roumanian Sports Club very shortly. After all, he would as soon sit over a cup of late tea with old John. There was something, indeed quite a lot of things, about this place he did not like, though the red-haired Patsy was certainly pretty and a figure quite in the adventurous tradition.

It was Patsy who reversed her glass, pulled a face, and said: "I'm thirsty. I'd like some champagne. Little gentleman, I'd like some champagne."

The little gentleman merely smiled vaguely. He had only four pounds with him, and he needed every shilling of it. Buying champagne had never been part of the adventures he had dreamed for himself. He had some notion of what it cost at this time of night, in such places. So he said nothing, braving Patsy's contempt.

"I'd like some bubbly too, dear," said Dot.

"Here, Luxy," cried the other girl, "what about it? I'd like some champagne."

"Ah, these girls," said Mr. Lux. He gave a final nod to his friend Meakin, and now rose from his seat. "Well, we'll have a bottle. Just give the order, Watson ol' man. Back in a minute." And off he went.

Hubert saw the waiter standing expectantly before him. "Er—let me see—what do you want?" he said to Patsy.

"The usual, George," the girl said to the waiter.

Hubert hoped the waiter would be a long time finding and opening the bottle, to give Mr. Lux every opportunity of returning. The waiter was back in a few minutes, however, and there were no signs of Mr. Lux. While he was filling the glasses, Meakin and the two girls looked about them casually and hummed.

"Two poundss five shillings, sare, if you pliss."

Hubert stared at him blankly.

"If you pliss," said the waiter firmly, looking Hubert straight in the eye.

"But—isn't it?—I mean—Mr. Lux," Hubert began stammering.

"Oh, my God!" cried Patsy, in utter scorn.

They were all looking at him now. There was no help for it. Hubert put down three pound notes, and found himself compelled to give the waiter five shillings as a tip. Two pounds ten! A stupid adventure this.

But he was thirsty, as well he might be, for by this time the Roumanian Sports Club was like an oven in which some very dubious meats had stayed too long. He gulped down his champagne, and then, feeling refreshed, careless, almost gay, he refilled his glass. It is hardly necessary to add that he had also to refill the glasses of his three companions, who were by no means shy drinkers. The wine did not seem to make Patsy any more friendly; she still looked at him out of narrowed eyes; and there was still something disconcerting about her smile. On the other hand, Dot was even more openly and outrageously amorous. Her arm, very plump and a trifle sticky, found its way round the back of his neck, and there was no way of disengaging it.

Somebody was staring hard at him. Hubert looked up and met the gaze of a young man in a blue suit who had just crossed the room. He was a young man with a hatchet face, an immense spread of shoulder, and unusually long arms and large hands; a very unpleasant-looking young man, uglier than Mr. Meakin. This fellow now stood before their table, and suddenly pushed his long neck out, so that his face came nearer and nearer.

"All right, Tommy, all right," cried Dot, her voice trembling a little.

Tommy's upper lip curled back derisively as he stared at Hubert. Then he made a noise like an angry rook: "Corrr!" looked them all over once more, and then left them.

"Tommy's bin pushing 'em back to-night," Mr. Meakin observed dispassionately, but with a sly glance at the two girls.

Hubert hastily drank some more champagne. He needed it, after making the acquaintance of Tommy. But he had not finished making acquaintances. There now arrived at the table one of the largest, fattest, and most disgusting women he had ever seen. Between two mountainous cheeks was set a little beak of a nose, and above that nose were two little hard and greedy eyes. Hubert disliked this woman at first sight. He was not to forget her in a hurry.

" 'Ello, 'ello, 'ello!" she cried, settling her enormous bulk in front of them. "Lookin' for you, my dear," she said to Dot. " 'Ow's tricks, Meaky?"

"Have a drink, Tiny?" said Dot, pushing over the bottle. "This is a pal of Luxy's, an' a very Nice Boy. Aren't you, deear?"

Hubert gave a sickly grin. It was time he was going home.

"Pleased to meet chew," said Tiny, leering at him. "But didn't catch the nime."

"Watson," Hubert mumbled, loathing her.

"Fancy that!" said Tiny, pouring some champagne into the nearest empty glass, apparently not caring whether anybody else had used it or not. "He's the spitten image of Teaser Charlie," she added, glancing at the others. "Isn't 'e, deear? Isn't 'e, Meaky?"

Hubert was quick enough to catch sight of Mr. Meakin making a face at her. "Never heard of him," said Mr. Meakin, frowning. At which Patsy laughed, not very pleasantly.

Before Hubert had time to do more than wonder vaguely
who Teaser Charlie might be, there rang through the room a
shrill whistle that stopped the piano and the dancing at once
and brought everybody to their feet. All the lights went out
except one above the door near them, which was at the opposite end of the room from the door Hubert had first entered.
There was an instant uproar and stampede, and tables, chairs
and glasses went flying. Hubert found himself being hurried
through the door, with Dot and Meakin at each side of him,
Dot still holding his arm. In another minute, they were all
hastening down a dimly-lit corridor, outside. He could feel
the immense Tiny behind, pressing against him, urging him
on. This must be a police raid. It could not be anything else.
All Hubert wanted to do now was get safely away, not merely
from the police but from all these queer people too; but there
seemed little chance of his doing that, for he did not know
where he was, and if he broke away from his companions now
he might find himself in the hands of the police. But, in any
case, it appeared as if his companions had no intention of
letting him go. He felt helpless, bewildered, and wished he
had never set foot in the Roumanian Sports Club.

Once at the end of the corridor, they turned to the right
and clattered down several flights of dark stairs. And now the
fresh night air was in his face, and he had a glimpse of the
stars. They seemed to be in a sort of mews.

"Well," Hubert began, "if you'll just tell me where I am,
I think I'll clear—"

"Shut up, you silly devil," Meakin whispered fiercely in his
ear. "Do you want us all copped?" He gripped Hubert's arm,
and then hurried him round to the left, in the shadow, until
at last they were in a side-street, where several small cars were
standing. Into one of these they were all bundled. Meakin

started it up at once and drove at a smart pace through a number of quiet streets. Once Hubert thought he caught a glimpse of the Euston Road.

They stopped outside some tall and mouldering apartment houses. Dot got out first, produced a key and opened the door of the nearest house. "Hurry up," she said.

Hubert hesitated. "I don't think I'll come in, thanks," he began.

Meakin caught his arm again. "Course you'll go in," he said menacingly. "If you don't, you'll be nabbed in a minute. Get inside quick, and don't talk so much."

Hubert was too frightened and bewildered to argue with him, though there did not seem any reason why he should not walk quietly away and go home. He followed Dot and the panting Tiny (Patsy had disappeared during the stampede) up four flights of stairs, with Meakin close behind him all the way.

"Welcome to my little abode, deeary," said Dot, and then disappeared into what was presumably a bedroom. The little abode consisted of these two rooms, and Hubert never remembered seeing a room he disliked more than the one in which he now found himself. It smelled of old blankets, cheap face powder, whisky, cigarettes, and cabbage water. The table and the floor were littered with dirty glasses, greasy plates, and cigarette ends. It was a horrible place. Hubert glanced at his watch. It was quarter to one. He might have been turning into bed now, after having had a cup of tea, a last gossip and a pipe with old John at the flat, which seemed at that moment a distant paradise. Meakin was prowling about the room, apparently looking for some whisky and cigarettes, for when he found them, he stopped prowling. He pushed them over to Hubert, with a sneering glance, but Hubert shook his head. So far as he was concerned, the night's festivities were over. He had had more than enough of this adventure.

Dot and Tiny reappeared, looking all the more repulsive now they were at home, and immediately pounced upon the cigarettes and the whisky, which they drank out of dirty tumblers with a little water added to it.

"Well, well," said Tiny, heaving a vast sigh as she settled in the only chair that could possibly accommodate her, "it's all in the game, isn't it? That knocks out the Rowmanians for a week or two, or for good. I was getting a bit tired of it, wasn't you, deear?"

Dot replied that she was, and might have enlarged upon the subject if Meakin, who did not appear to be at his ease, had not held up a hand. " 'Ear that?" he said softly.

They all listened intently, staring at one another. Some-body was coming up the stairs. Dot ran forward and switched off the light. They all sat, breathing heavily, in the darkness. Hubert felt almost suffocated. He could hear his heart pounding away.

The footsteps stopped outside the door. A key turned in the lock. "No, you don't. No, you don't," said a voice, trium-phantly, and then the light was switched on, and Hubert saw that two men were standing in the doorway. One of them was the sinister Tommy. The other was a taller and older man with a hooked nose and a slight squint. They came forward, closing the door behind them.

"Didn't expect us, I dare say," said the older man, grinning at them. "Quite a treat, this unexpected visit. Oh no, Meaky, you don't," he cried, as Meakin made a little movement. "You'll stand over there and you'll stand still." And his hand slid out of his pocket and showed something black and shiny. An automatic.

Dot gave a little scream. Tiny sat up, her little eyes bright and watchful. Meakin shrugged his shoulders, then stood motionless. "What's the idea, Jarvey?" he said huskily.

"You know the idea, Meaky," said Mr. Jarvey. "I know you've got 'em. You can't get away with it. Tommy here was watching Luxy."

"That's right," said Tommy, with a grin.

"I'm not so sure Luxy didn't tip them for the raid, so you could get away with it," Mr. Jarvey went on meditatively, "but it won't do, won't do at all. You've just had time to put 'em away, but I don't think you have done. Come on, you pancake-faced bleeder," he added, with sudden and startling ferocity, "bring 'em out, quick, or I'll flatten you."

"I haven't got 'em," muttered Meakin. "Never 'ad 'em."

"Go through him, Tommy," said Mr. Jarvey. Then he looked at Hubert. "Hello, what's this? Teaser?"

"No, it isn't," Tiny put in, ingratiatingly. "Like 'im, isn't it?"

"His name's Watson," said Dot. "Luxy brought him to the club."

"He did, did he." Mr. Jarvey looked at Hubert as a very large snake might look at a very small rabbit. "Friend of Luxy's, eh? Come here, you. Where do you come in, eh? Come on, spit it out."

Hubert tried to reply, but by this time Mr. Jarvey was engaged in bringing the automatic to about an inch from his nose, so that Hubert was busy swallowing hard.

"Nothing there, Tommy?" cried Mr. Jarvey, still humorously wagging the gun in Hubert's face. "All right, we'll try this fellow before we go any further. Come on, Dr. Watson, empty your pockets quick. Help him, Tommy. He's shivering so hard he'll be a week getting through them."

Everything in Hubert's pockets was tumbled out on the table, his note-case, watch, cigarette-case, two or three letters, and—to his amazement—a small wash-leather bag. It did not belong to him, this bag; he had never seen it before.

Mr. Jarvey grabbed hold of it, tipped the contents into his palm. Hubert saw the flash and sparkle of jewels there, for one second, before Mr. Jarvey returned the gems to the bag and put the bag itself in his pocket.

"I don't know—how it came—to be there," Hubert gasped. "Honestly, I don't."

"You don't know how it came to be there," sneered Tommy, and put an enormous fist within an inch of Hubert's chin. Hubert stepped back and the fist followed him.

Mr. Jarvey now took a hand in the game. He came forward and thrust his face at Hubert. "Who gave you that bag? Come on now, chicken-face. Who brought you into the job, eh? Say something, you little rat."

"Let me pug him one," Tommy pleaded, doubling his fist again. "That'll start him talking, if it doesn't send him to sleep."

"I tell you I don't know anything about it," cried Hubert, almost tearfully now. And he began a confused account of how he met Mr. Lux at the coffee-stall and was taken by him to the Roumanian Sports Club.

Mr. Jarvey stopped him. "I see," he said, and it was evident that he did see, for he gave Mr. Meakin a sidelong dark look. "A bit of planting, eh, Meaky, in case you were stopped? Was it your little idea or Lux's? Anyhow, we'll soon know. You come with us, Meaky. And as for you," he turned to Hubert, "the sooner your mother gives you a spanking and puts you to bed, the better. But don't let me see you about again, young feller-me-lad, or you'll learn something."

"That is so," said Tommy, who as he went past contrived to give Hubert a shove with his shoulder that nearly knocked the wretched youth off his feet. Then the door closed behind the three men.

And now at last the two women found their tongues.

Dot looked Hubert up and down. "You're a nice one, aren't you?" she screamed, the image of outraged virtue. "Startin' your bother here after we'd looked after you!"

Tiny took up the theme. "If I'd 'ad my way, 'e'd bin left to look after hisself. You're too soft, that's what it is my deear. That soft 'eart of yours 'ull get you into trouble yet." She looked, at Hubert with mountainous disfavour. "Ought to be ashamed of yourself."

"I should think so indeed," said Dot, tossing her head. "How I'm going to live this down, I don't know."

This was too much for Hubert. He had stood enough from the men. "Oh, shut up," he mumbled. "You know very well I haven't done anything. I'm going." He went to the table to collect the contents of his pockets, which were still lying there.

But Tiny, big as she was, proved herself too quick for him. "Oh no, you don't, you don't," she cried, with the same unpleasant intonation that Jarvey had given the phrase. She put her hands over the heap of things. "Just a minute, just a minute, young feller!"

"Give me those things," cried Hubert, tears of vexation in his eyes. He tugged at her great arm.

"You lay a finger on her," said Dot, jumping up, "and you'll get something that'll last you some time."

Hubert sullenly retreated. "I want to go. Give me those things."

The fat horrible woman was now holding up his letters. "Calls hisself Watson," she cried, triumphantly. "An' what do

I see 'ere? All to Hubert Graham, Esquire." One of the letters had been addressed to him at the flat, the other to the office. She read out both addresses. "Passin' hisself off under false names, an' then tryin' to get girls into trouble. That's 'is game."

"And a damn dirty game too," said Dot, with righteous indignation.

" 'E'll 'ave to pay for it, that's all," said Tiny coolly, and before he could interfere she had taken the remaining notes from his case. "One pound ten shillings, that's all 'e's got, an' calls hisself a gentleman." She flung down the empty case.

"Leave it alone, you—you—rotten old thief," Hubert screamed.

But now she was actually looking at the letters, one of which was from his parents in the country. "There's some people'ud be surprised to learn about 'is goings on," she observed with relish, "an' thirty bob's not goin' to pay us for all the trouble 'e's caused us, is it, my deear?"

"It isn't," replied Dot, "but we mustn't be too hard upon him. He's young. That's a nice watch, deear. Perhaps if he gave you that, you'd give him his letters back."

"It's lettin' him off too light," said the other harpy, taking up the watch, "but if that's 'ow you feel about it, deear." And she threw over the letters, which Hubert instantly crammed into his overcoat pocket. Then he snatched up his keys, note-case, and cigarette-case. "You—you—give me my watch," he demanded, in a quavering voice.

Tiny leered at him, "Hubert Graham, Esquire, calling hisself Watson," she began, and at the same time Dot opened the door. "You get out of here quick as you can, whatever your name is, or you'll get yourself into some more bother. And mind Tommy isn't waiting for you at the bottom of the steps, just where it's dark. Anyhow, he'll be back in a minute, so you can wait for him—if you really *must* see him."

Hubert fled, and the last thing he heard, as the door closed behind him, was a harsh scream of laughter. He knew they were laughing at him, and knew that he deserved to be laughed at, and that was the last bitter drop in the cup of his misery.

It was some time before he found the Euston Road, and it was weary way, trudging along, tired out, in his thin dress shoes, back to the flat, where he might have been sitting at his ease, two hours ago, with four pounds and a watch in his pocket and his self-respect intact.

John was still up, a book and an empty cup in front of him. "Hello, young Hube! Lord, but it's late. What have you been up to, you look all out? Here, hang on, and I'll brew another spot of tea. You could do some, couldn't you?"

"Yes, thanks," said Hubert faintly. He stretched himself out in a chair, safe at home at last.

HANDEL AND THE RACKET

There must have been a great many absurd discussions and arguments taking place on that particular afternoon in the City of London. But these two men must have been engaged in the oddest and drollest. To begin with, they were complete strangers to one another, and then they were busy arguing somewhere in the middle of a vertical tunnel or shaft in a very tall building not far from Cheapside.

It was one of those lifts that you work—rather dubiously, as a rule—for yourself. The tall, bony man had entered it on the highest floor it reached, where he had been visiting Grossman and Jenkins', wholesale shirtings, on behalf of a certain provincial organisation known as the Luddenstall Co-operative Society. The lift began its descent, but was checked at the next floor below, where the second lift-traveller was rather ceremoniously ushered in by the manager of the United Tropical Products, Ltd. This second man was neither tall nor bony. He was in a comfortable late middle age, had a large clean-shaven face and a sedentary figure, looked wealthy and American, and, like many men who are wealthy and American, he looked as if he had been kept in cold storage for several years. He entered the lift, nodded to the manager of the United Tropical Products, who closed the two gates, and then, without paying any attention to the tall, bony man, pressed the button marked "Ground Floor."

The lift moved a few yards, hesitated, moved a few more yards, then came to a stop somewhere between floors. The American gentleman frowned at the button marked "Ground Floor" and pressed it again. Nothing happened.

"Did you push it hard enough?" the tall, bony man asked, in a marked Yorkshire accent.

"I did," replied the other, dryly.

The tall man applied an outsize and capable-looking forefinger to the button, but he too had no success.

"Satisfied?" the American inquired, with an ironical inflexion that seemed to come easily to his deep and rather harsh voice.

"I am," said his companion, not at all disconcerted, "but I wouldn't ha' been if I hadn't had a go myself. Seems to have stuck somewhere. We'd better see if we can go up a bit and then try to come down. What d'you say?"

The American nodded and pressed the necessary button. But the lift had decided to stay where it was. The two passengers put their noses to the gate, and heard a voice coming up the shaft. They shouted to it, but it made no reply. After a minute or two, however, they heard another voice, much louder and more authoritative, addressing them. "It's all right," the voice bellowed at them. "We'll have it working in a few minutes. Don't touch anything till I tell you to. Do you hear me?"

They roared in unison that they did hear him.

"All right, then," it replied. "Shan't be long."

The American and the tall, bony man looked at one another. "All right, eh?" said the former, sticking out his under-lip, not unlike a very large, pale baby. "All wrong, I call it."

"Aye, it's a nuisance," said the Yorkshireman, whose name was Hebblethwaite. He did not seem to be very much put out by the delay, and his assent was mere friendliness. "Oldish lift, this, I should say."

"Very old pattern. Ought to have been scrapped years ago. One of your antiques, this elevator," said the American, withdrawing his under-lip now in order to produce a slight smile. "Well, I'm glad this isn't the Chrysler Building in New York."

"I thought you were an American," said the other, as if congratulating himself on his perspicacity.

"Yes, I'm an American." He hesitated a moment, then added, with the formal politeness of his kind: "My name is Ongar, sir."

"Tom Hebblethwaite's mine."

"Very pleased to make your acquaintance, Mr. Hebblethwaite," said Mr. Ongar, smiling. Then, as if recollecting that he was a person of great importance and authority—and there was something about him that suggested he was all that—he frowned, brought out a pocket-book, and frowned still harder into some of its pages. He continued to do this while Mr. Hebblethwaite filled and lit his pipe and puffed away at it quite contentedly. Then, after two or three minutes of silence between these two gentlemen in mid-air, Mr. Ongar, still looking at his list of engagements or his notes, began to whistle, very softly.

Mr. Hebblethwaite let his companion whistle for about a minute, then interrupted him. "Now I'll tell you what it is you're trying to whistle," he announced heartily.

Mr. Ongar looked up from his little book. "I didn't know I was whistling."

"Well you *were* whistling, an' I'll tell you what it was—an' I don't suppose there's another chap i' this building could do that."

"What was it?"

"It's an air from Handel's *Judas Maccabaeus*," Mr. Hebblethwaite told him, triumphantly.

Though Mr. Ongar had said that he didn't know he had been whistling, nevertheless the tune must have been still running through his head, for he whistled a little more of it. Then his large, pale face suddenly lit up, turning him at once into an enthusiast. "You're right, Mr.—er—Hebblethwaite," he cried, "it's an air from *Judas Maccabaeus*. And if anybody had told me that here, in this building in the City of London, that toon would have been recognized as slickly as that I wouldn't have believed them. You know Handel's moosic? Well, that's fine. Handel, in my o-pinion, is *the* greatest of all *the* great moosicians of all time. Yes, sir, *the* greatest. And you know Handel's o-ra-torios?"

"Handel! I should think I do know Handel," cried Mr. Hebblethwaite. "An' if you'd been in t'Luddenstall Choral Society as long as I have *you'd* know Handel an' all. I've sung Handel till I've been nearly black i' t'face. Why—bless my soul!—we know Handel backwards up our way."

"That's fine." And Mr. Ongar beamed.

"But I'll tell you one thing," Mr. Hebblethwaite continued, friendly but aggressive. "You didn't get that tune right, y'know. That's why I mentioned it."

Mr. Ongar was shocked. "Now if there's one thing I bee-lieve I can pride myself on having," he said, very slowly and deliberately, "it's an ear for moosic, and especially the moosic of Handel. If I whistled that toon, sir, you can bet your life that toon was right the way I whistled it."

"I wouldn't bet tuppence on it, nivver mind my life," cried the Yorkshireman. "Nay, you got it wrong. An' I'll show you where you got it wrong an' all." And without any more ado he produced his own version of the air, humming it in a not unpleasant baritone and beating time.

The other shook his head. "You're wrong. I'm not saying a thing against that toon. Glad to have heard it. But that is *no-ot* the air that Handel wrote for *Judas Maccabaeus*. I don't know what I whistled before, because I was thinking about something else, but I'll whistle it now and you'll hear just exactly where you went all wrong." And very solemnly Mr. Ongar puckered up his chubby mouth and whistled, at the same time marking the beat of the music on his companion's coat-sleeve.

It was now Mr. Hebblethwaite's turn to shake his head, and he took full advantage of it. After that the two enthusiasts, remote from the world in their suspended cage, began to argue warmly, and it is doubtful if either of them remembered where he was. They were too busy trying to crush each other with a statement of their several qualifications, and as neither of them could be called modest, they were very busy indeed.

"I tell you," Mr. Hebblethwaite would say, bringing his face down to within nine inches of Mr. Ongar's and tapping him repeatedly, "t'Luddenstall Choral Society—and, mind you, though Luddenstall's not so big, you'll go a long way afore you find a better choral society—and, as I say, t'Luddenstall Choral's given *Judas* three times now, and I've had it dinned into me that many times, I know it as well as I know my own name."

"I didn't say anything bee-fore," cried Mr. Ongar, "but you're talking now to James Stark Ongar—head of Ongar Tropical Products. Keep that to yourself, because I don't want a noise started round this little trip of mine to this side. But now you know who I am, you'll know that for the last ten years I've been putting up the dollars for the Ongar Handel Festival, the biggest moosical festival of modern times."

"And when owd Joe Clough—that's our conductor—tells you you've got to learn summat, you've got to learn it. There's no hanky-panky about it. When t'Luddenstall Choral gives an oratorio, they don't just have a bit of a pop at it, hit or miss like, they *learn* it—up and down an' sideways. An' we haven't given *Judas* once—we've given it *three times*——"

"And just let me tell you a thing. I've got *the* finest collection of Handel manuscripts and letters—not the finest in America, but the finest in the *world*. You're talking now to a man who's given the best of his time—outside business—and a real lot of his dollars to the moosic of Handel, a man who's had the greatest conductors staying right there in his own house in Noo York, to talk to him about Handel. And when I whistle a toon of Handel's, I get it right. I couldn't get it wrong if I tried."

Still talking like this, they suddenly found themselves at the bottom of the lift-shaft, with a commissionaire and a man in overalls opening the gates for them and entering into elaborate explanations of the delay. But Messrs. Ongar and Hebblethwaite brushed aside these fellows and their chatter. They were no longer interested in lifts. They were still busy with their argument. Both talking at once, they walked forward into the street, where a large hired Rolls-Royce was waiting for the American.

The sight of this car gave Mr. Ongar an idea. "Just listen to me, Mr. Hebblethwaite," he said, with more than his usual emphasis. "You're a busy man. So am I—and you don't know how busy. But we've just got to get this thing settled. Over in my suite at the Palatial I've got a score of *Judas Maccabaeus*—bought it only two days ago—an eighteenth-century score, large as life—and we'll drive there right now and get this thing settled. I'd hate to spend the rest of this day without proving to you how wrong you are. What do you say?"

"That'll do me champion," said Mr. Hebblethwaite. "We'll have a look at that air on paper, and if I'm wrong you can call me all t'names you can think of. But I sha'n't be."

They drove off at once to the Palatial, one of the super-*de-luxe* hotels of which Mr. Hebblethwaite had often heard but had never visited. He was suitably impressed by its green and gold splendour. "By gow, it'll cost a pretty penny staying i' this place," he remarked, as they went soaring in yet another lift towards Mr. Ongar's suite.

"I reckon it's about the best you've got," said Mr. Ongar, casually. "Very comfortable. And not too big."

"That's right," replied the Yorkshireman, ironically. "Not too big. What you might call homely. Nobbut about the size of a smallish town, that's all. You might get lost in it, but, on t'other hand, you'd nivver be more than half a mile out."

Mr. Ongar led the way into a green and gold sitting-room. "Sit down, Mr. Hebblethwaite," he said, not without a trace of irony. "Make yourself comfortable, because in one moment I'm going to prove to you that you were wrong about that toon. Now here's the score." He went to the table and picked up a large calf-bound volume. And that is all he did do, in the matter of *Judas Maccabaeus*, for some time, because at that moment something happened.

"Well, well, well!" cried a voice in most unpleasant, sneering tones.

Two young men came through the doorway that obviously led into the bedroom, and one of them immediately planted himself in front of the door that Mr. Hebblethwaite had just closed, the door that communicated with the rest of the hotel. The other young man suddenly barked "Stick 'em up!" and produced a very, nasty-looking automatic. Messrs. Ongar and Hebblethwaite found themselves with their hands in the air, and the young man with the automatic very swiftly and deftly tapped all their pockets and appeared to be very pleased to discover that these two gentlemen were not in the habit of carrying firearms.

Mr. Hebblethwaite felt that he had been plunged into the middle of a talkie. He had made the acquaintance of young men who moved and talked like this in the Luddenstall Plaza, to which he frequently took Mrs. Hebblethwaite in their hours of ease. He had always enjoyed the crook dramas of Hollywood, but had always considered them somewhat unreal. Now he hastily revised this judgment. These two young men were real enough, and yet they might have walked straight out of a talkie. They were gorgeously arrayed in vivid striped suits, startling ties, and loud shoes, and were clearly very proud of their appearance. They suggested a pair of sinister peacocks. But there was nothing really youthful about their swagger. They had not the faces of young men. They had the faces of men who had not many years to their credit, but who looked far older than they ought to have simply because it was almost miraculous that they should have lived as long as they had. The one who stood in front of the door was the less objectionable of the two, though, he was the bigger and burlier. There was something peculiarly detestable about the smaller one with the automatic. He had waved black hair, a face of so pale an olive shade that it looked almost green, very hard little eyes, and a cruel twisted mouth. The longer Mr. Hebblethwaite looked at him, the more he forgave Hollywood for what it had done in its crook dramas.

"Well, well, well!" this fellow drawled again, speaking only from one side of his mouth. "You look surprised to see me, Mr. James Stark Ongar."

Here he was only speaking the truth. Ongar *did* look surprised to see him. "I don't understand this. What's the idea? Who are you?"

The man at the door laughed hoarsely at this. "Just a coupla' guys making a nice trip like yourself, Mr. Ongar," he said, with evident relish of his wit.

"I'll do this, Sam," said the smaller and darker young man, with a warning glance. Then he went nearer to Mr. Ongar, and almost sneered in his face. "I'll tell you a little secret Mr. Ongar. Just to show yuh what a big surprise it is. I'm Charlie Banetti."

Mr. Ongar started, almost jumped. "Banetti!" he gasped, staring at the other. "What are you doing here?"

"Can't I have a little trip, too?" inquired Mr. Banetti, showing his teeth. Then, very dramatically, he changed his tone. "You don't know me, eh? But you know all about me, eh? Yeah, and I know all about you. Mr. James Stark Ongar— one of the leaders of the big clean-up movement. Well, you've not cleaned Charlie Banetti up yet, have you, you big bohunk? And I came over on the same boat, just to give you a little surprise. We'll do some cleaning-up on this side, only I'll do the cleaning."

"That's so," said Sam at the door, still enjoying himself.

"Don't move," cried Mr. Banetti.

"Here, I say," said Mr. Hebblethwaite, who felt it was time he took a hand in this. "Hadn't you better put that thing away?"

Mr. Banetti gave him one swift, contemptuous glance.

"You might let it off, y'know," Mr. Hebblethwaite continued, earnestly. "And i' this country we hang fowk that's careless wi' them things."

Mr. Banetti now produced a sneer more dreadful than any he had contrived before. It was so huge and ferocious that it must have hurt his face. He fixed his cold little eyes on Mr. Hebblethwaite. "Oh, yer do, eh? Well, who told you to come to life? You're dumb, anyhow, and you'll stay dumb." And, saying this, he stepped forward, and with one contemptuous flick of his finger brought Mr. Hebblethwaite's tie out of his waistcoat. "Any more cracks from you, big boy, and I'll sock you so hard you won't know what country you're in." He gave Mr. Hebblethwaite one prod in the stomach with the blunt muzzle of the automatic. "Get in there," he commanded. "Go on, move."

Mr. Hebblethwaite found himself in the bedroom, with the door shut in his face. He was angrier than he had been for a long time. Mr. Banetti's methods had left him in a fury. Especially was he enraged by that little matter of the pulled-out tie. You cannot pull out a Luddenstall man's tie in that fashion—not, that is, if you are a stranger, and a sneering American gangster at that—and reasonably expect nothing to happen. For the moment, however, Mr. Hebblethwaite stayed dumb. He examined the bedroom, but though quite a charming apartment, admirably decorated in the familiar green-and-gold manner, it did not give him any satisfaction. The bedroom window did not face the same way as the sitting-room window. It merely looked out on a sort of white-tiled court. There was no fire-escape or any other kind of escape. There were, of course, various bells in the room, but when Mr. Hebblethwaite troubled to examine them, he vastly underrated Mr. Banetti's technique. The bells had been thoroughly put out of order. There was now no means of communication between the bedroom and the rest of the hotel. Apart from the door into the sitting-room, there was only one other door, and that led to the bathroom, a very fine bathroom indeed, but offering no chance of escape, except by way of the waste-pipes. After spending a minute or two looking round him, Mr. Hebblethwaite decided on a plan of action. He looked quiet enough now; but actually he was still very angry. No doubt another Luddenstall man would have recognised the signs.

He began putting his plan into action by scribbling something on a sheet of hotel note-paper, pocketing a piece of soap from the bathroom, and then banging hard upon the door into the sitting-room. Evidently this banging disturbed Mr. Banetti, for it was not long before he threw open the door and asked what the hell was meant by it.

"I want to come out of here," Mr. Hebblethwaite told him.

"Oh yeah?" cried Mr. Banetti, quite in the traditional manner. "You want to come out, do yuh? Well, listen to me, you long dummy. If you stay in there and stay quiet, you won't get hurt. If you don't, you will. You look like a hick to me, and you sound like one, and I never did like small-town stuff, so I don't want to sock you. But keep butting in, and you'll wonder what hit you, Reuben."

"Aye, but you see it's like this," said Mr. Hebblethwaite, eagerly. "I came here wi' Mr. Ongar 'cos we had an argument and wanted to settle it by looking at some music he's got.

Well, you might let us settle it and get done wi' it afore you start yours. Won't tak' a minute, an' Mr. Ongar'll be a lot easier to deal wi' when he's got this off his mind."

"And then you think we're going to let you walk out, I suppose?" said Mr. Banetti, with cutting sarcasm. "Where d'yuh think we come from? Don't worry. You're staying here a long time yet."

"No, it isn't that," said Mr. Hebblethwaite, truthfully. "I just want to get it settled, that's all. I'll come back here then, and be as quiet as you like."

"I'll say you will," Mr. Banetti retorted, grimly. Then he said, over his shoulder: "This right, Ongar?"

"That's right," said Mr. Ongar, wearily. "We'd had an argument about some music, and we came here to see which of us was right."

"And you see, mister," said Mr. Hebblethwaite, quite humbly, to the gangster, "I've written what I think it is on a bit o' paper. An' if you'll just let me look at the music—for half a minute, that's all—I'll give Mr. Ongar the paper if I'm right, and I'll just throw it away if I'm wrong—and that's all. Nowt on it. But I know Mr. Ongar'll be easier in his mind and 'ull tak' more notice of you when it's fairly settled."

"Mr. Ongar's going to take a lot of notice of me—more than he's ever done—right now," Mr. Banetti drawled; then added, contemptuously: "All right. Snap into it."

Mr. Hebblethwaite snapped into it by walking over to the table, opening the large calf-bound score, and comparing it with the paper he produced from his pocket. "Well, by gow!— would you believe it!" he cried, apparently both vexed and ashamed. "You wor right an' I wor wrong, Mr. Ongar. I'll throw this away afore you see it an' laugh at me." And he walked to the open window and dropped the paper out of it.

A second later, there appeared to be a noise below, almost as if the paper had suddenly acquired much greater weight and had hit something.

"You see," said Mr. Hebblethwaite, humbly, as he returned to Mr. Banetti's side, still holding the score open with one hand, "I don't know if you're interested i' music, but this tune here——" And he held the score open for Mr. Banetti's inspection.

The gangster had to give it a glance. Nobody could have resisted one short look. And the moment that Mr. Banetti chose to glance at the score was the identical moment in which Mr. Hebblethwaite turned himself from a slow simpleton into a lightning man of action, for a man may wear spectacles and be a buyer for a co-operative society and yet be a man of action, and there was once a Sergeant Hebblethwaite of the West Yorks Regiment who had won a D.C.M. on the Somme. At the end of that moment the automatic was no longer in Mr. Banetti's possession, and Mr. Banetti himself was reeling back, the victim of a sudden and vigorous blow delivered with a substantial Handel score.

"Hold on to that," cried Mr. Hebblethwaite sharply to Mr. Ongar, at the same time throwing him the automatic. "Watch t'other chap." Mr. Hebblethwaite then swiftly removed his spectacles, and turned his attention to Mr. Banetti, who was still a little dazed.

"Na, lad," he said, grimly. "You an' me's going to have a bit of a do. We've got summat to settle. Don't you interfere wi' this, Mr. Ongar. Watch t'other chap. Na then, lad, let's see who's going to do t'socking."

The gangster was game enough, and, having been brought up in a tough school, he could fight. He was younger than Mr. Hebblethwaite, but too many late nights and too much bad liquor had withered away the advantage of that difference. Moreover, Mr. Hebblethwaite, having been brought up in a fairly tough school himself, could also fight, and he was heavier and much longer in the reach. The battle only lasted about four minutes, but during that time Mr. Banetti was thoroughly socked.

"And nar I'll pull thy tie aht lad," roared Mr. Hebblethwaite, broader than ever in his accent now; and as the gangster went staggering back for the last time, Mr. Hebblethwaite sprang forward and gave that innocent piece of silk such a savage jerk that it split, and the tie came away with his hand. And Luddenstall honour was satisfied.

At this point it looked as if Sam was ready, in spite of the gun in Mr. Ongar's hand, to play some part in the game, but, unfortunately for him, a very surprising thing happened. The door behind him suddenly opened, and before Sam could do anything dramatic, and long before his leader could collect himself, there were four other people in the room—namely, one assistant-manager, two porters, and a very large policeman. True to the traditions of this curiously old-fashioned island, where a certain narrowness of view towards such people as Mr. Banetti still exists, the policeman was very unsympathetic in his attitude towards these two distinguished visitors, and was instrumental in removing them to a place where various charges were preferred against them.

"But what I don't see," said Mr. Hebblethwaite, half an hour later, "is what they were after." He was smoking a cigar of magnificent flavour and proportions.

Mr. Ongar removed from his lips a companion colossus. "Well, I reckon it was a noo racket," he said, slowly. "Banetti knew I was one of the men prominent in the clean-up movement, to drive the gangs out of business. If he'd have made me sign a cheque right here in London, I'd have looked mighty small, and he'd have had the laugh as well as the dollars. And he had the cheque all ready for me to sign. They'd have tied us up, cashed the cheque within ten minutes, and been out of the country to-night, over to Paris or Berlin. But thanks to you, Mr. Hebblethwaite, we never got that far."

"Aye, that lad did himself in wi' me when he went an' pulled my tie aht," said Mr. Hebblethwaite, ruminating.

"But how did you get those folks, the porters and the police, up here?" Mr. Ongar asked. "Did you shout when you were in the bedroom?"

The Yorkshireman grinned. "Nar that wor a neat bit o' work, though I must say I nivver thought it 'ud come off. When I first come in here, I looked out o' t'window an' noticed a sort o' glass veranda at bottom. So I writes a bit of a message—telling 'em there's dirty work up i' this room—and you saw me throw it out. Only I'd wrapped it round a big piece o' soap and it stuck champion. I thought to myself either it'll smash that glass or it'll give it a good bang, an' onnyway somebody'll tak' notice. As they did. I couldn't throw it out o' t'bedroom, you see, 'cos that window isn't above owt and nobody'd ha' seen t'paper."

Mr. Ongar paid his tribute to this neat bit of work, then looked very solemnly at his companion. "Mr. Hebblethwaite," he began, rather as if he was addressing him at a public dinner and proposing his health, "you're the sort of executive we want in Ongar Tropical Products. What about it? Name your terms?"

"D'you know, I've heard 'em talk like that monny a time on t'pictures," cried Mr. Hebblethwaite with enthusiasm, "an' I always thought it wor a lot o' blather, but—by gow!—nar it's happened to me. Well, thanks very much, Mr. Ongar, but I can't tak' it on. You see, I'm t'sort o' chap they want in t'Luddenstall Co-op. an' all. I don't say I couldn't do wi' a bit more money, but best thing you can do is to write an' tell 'em so."

"I feel very, very grateful, Mr. Hebblethwaite," said the American, apparently beginning another public speech.

Mr. Hebblethwaite cut him short. "Nar I see you want to do summat an' you don't know what. You're ower here a bit, aren't you? Always coming and going like? Aye. Well, you mun promise me to come an' hear our Luddenstall Choral give t'*Messiah*—you'll hear a right bit o' good Handel singing an' if you enjoy yourself, well, put your hand down an' give t'Luddenstall Choral a right good subscription. We can do wi' a good patron."

"I will," said Mr. Ongar, eagerly. "Glad to do it now." Then he smiled mischievously. "But don't forget that I was right about that toon from *Judas Maccabaeus*."

Mr. Hebblethwaite jumped to his feet. "Nay—by gow!— you weren't. Don't get that into your head. I only said I wor wrong just to get that bit o' paper out o' t'window. Bless my soul!—I knew I were right all time. Here," he continued aggressively, picking up the score, "just try whistling that. You'll soon see who's right."

We leave them whistling.

AN ARABIAN NIGHT IN PARK LANE

The Most Honourable the Marquess of Gairloch, Charles William Edmund Alexander Gordon-Fitzstewart, K.G., P.C., G.C.V.O., and Helen Victoria Mary Christina, his Marchioness, were At Home. They were At Home at Gairloch House to all the political and social luminaries of the town. The lower half of Park Lane looked like a particularly congested motor show of particularly large and expensive cars. Two linkmen stood at the bottom of the steps. Inside the hall was a double row of enormous footmen, who looked as if at any moment they would burst into a baritone chorus. In spite of the special police who kept moving things and people on, a large number of proletarians, mostly feminine, stood as near as possible to the steps and peeped through the great open doorway, fully convinced, no doubt, that this was better than paying money to see a musical comedy. The large and expensive cars deposited the social and political luminaries in great quantities, and these important personages passed in a glittering stream up the steps, through the hall, and then up the noble twin staircases that curved towards their hostess. Lady Gairloch smiled at them all. She was wearing all the family jewels, and though a not unhandsome middle-aged woman, she was so bejewelled and bright that she looked more like a successful Christmas-tree than a human being. After passing their hostess, the guests moved on into the enormous library and the drawing-room. Both these apartments seemed to be full of people, yet the twin staircases, the hall below, the steps outside, were not empty of new guests, who came on in a steady stream. It was a tremendous affair.

In a corner of the library, not so crowded as the rest of the room was, two men were standing very close together, talking in whispers. They both looked wrong. Their dress-suits did not fit them very well. They were not wearing any crosses or ribbons. One of them was tall, bony, and spectacled, and the other was very short and broad, with a face like raw steak, and enormous rough hands. This short man, however, had a perfect right to be there. He had been invited. He was, in fact, one of the somebodies, being Joseph Puddaby, the Trade Union leader, Member of Parliament for the Luddenstall Division in the West Riding, and formerly one of His Majesty's Ministers. The tall man was a fraud. His name could not have been found on Lady Gairloch's guest list. He was Mr. Tom Hebblethwaite, buyer for the Luddenstall Co-operative Society, in London on one of his frequent business trips. The dress-suit he was wearing—or partly wearing, for it was a shocking misfit—had been hired that very afternoon, when his friend, Joe Puddaby, had suggested that he should attend this reception, making use of the invitation card bearing the name of one of Joe's colleagues in the Labour Party, Jack

Moorman, a grim proletarian who would have nothing to do with such hospitalities of the idle class. Mr. Hebblethwaite, curious as to what high society looked like, had allowed himself to be persuaded into this adventure, but he had been dubious about it. He still looked dubious.

"But you know, Joe," he was whispering, "when that chap called out 'Mr. John Moorman' and I had to go up and answer to it, I got in a fair sweat. I thought: 'What if somebody pops out and says I'm not Jack Moorman?' I'd ha' been in a nice mess."

"Oh, it's nowt," replied Mr. Puddaby. "There's so many here and it's all such a mess, they nivver know who's who. Don't you bother about that. Just tak' it all in while you are here. I thought you might as well see a do like this. There won't be so many more," he added, grimly. "We'll see to that."

Mr. Hebblethwaite looked about him. Most of the people were completely unknown to him, but there was a sprinkling of political celebrities whom he recognised from their photographs and caricatures in the press. Indeed, this affair was something between a theatrical scene in the grand manner and a political cartoon that had come to life. It was all very odd and bewildering. Mr. Hebblethwaite would have enjoyed it more, though, if he had not been conscious of the fact that he was there under false pretences. This was his first intimate glimpse of high society, and so far he had not formed a very high opinion of it. A few, a very few, of the men looked really distinguished, and here and there were some beautiful women. But most of the women, even the very handsome ones, were too elaborately got up, too painted and bediamonded, for his taste. He made a few mental notes for the benefit of Mrs. Hebblethwaite, who would want to know all the details when he came to tell her about this party.

"I'll tell you what it is, Joe," he remarked. "If you take a good look at this lot—and don't bother about clothes and jewels they're wearing—they don't seem any better than t'folk you see at a Luddenstall chapel bazaar."

"They don't look as good, lad," replied Mr. Puddaby, chuckling.

"Yond old woman there'ud make a good advertisement for enamel, wouldn't she?" said Mr. Hebblethwaite.

At this moment Mr. Puddaby was wanted by a political colleague of the highest importance, and he had to leave his friend. Left alone, Mr. Hebblethwaite felt very uneasy. Most of the guests obviously knew most of the other guests, so people stood about talking in groups. If they moved from one room to another, as they frequently did, they did this in groups too. It was not pleasant being alone, and it was still less pleasant when you knew that you ought not to be there at all. Mr. Hebblethwaite moved about a bit, and tried to look, as solitary people often do try to look at parties, as if he was simply on his way to rejoin a vast group of friends in some distant corner. Once an elderly woman with hollow, rouged cheeks, and a tremendous curved nose, rushed across to him and gave a little screech of recognition.

"How d'you do?" said Mr. Hebblethwaite, bewildered, for he had never seen this intimidating female before in his life.

No sooner had he opened his mouth than she realised that she had made a mistake. Her mouth closed with a snap. Her eyes froze in a ghastly and glacial fashion. And without a word of explanation or apology, she quickly turned away, leaving Mr. Hebblethwaite staring at her retreating shoulder-blades, which reminded him of plucked fowls. He told the shoulder-blades very quietly what he thought about them and their owner. It was then that he first encountered the large man with the soldierly moustache.

"Excuse me," said the large man, staring hard at Mr. Hebblethwaite, "are you Mr. Corcoran?"

"No, I'm not," said Mr. Hebblethwaite, who did not like the look of this large man with the soldierly moustache. He did not look like an ordinary guest. There was something vaguely official about him, though he was wearing full evening dress.

"Ah! There's a message for him, that's all," said the large man. "You don't mind my asking, do you? You're like him, but I see the difference now. You're—er—mister—er——?" And he waited for the name to be filled in.

The query left Mr. Hebblethwaite with the alternative of refusing to give his name, which might look awkward, or, if he did give it, with the further alternative of calling himself Moorman or Hebblethwaite. If he called himself Moorman, there was a possibility that this man might know Moorman. If he gave his proper name, he declared himself an uninvited guest. That would probably not matter, so he risked it. "Hebblethwaite's my name," he muttered.

"Quite so, Mr. Hebblethwaite," said the large man, who then nodded and walked away.

Mr. Hebblethwaite promptly moved off in the opposite direction. There was something about this large man, something about his soldierly moustache and his staring eyes, that he did not like. Five minutes later, as he stood in a corner idly watching the chattering throng, he felt that somebody was staring at him. He took a quick glance round, then saw, between two groups, about ten yards away, that soldierly moustache and those eyes. And the eyes were fixed speculatively on him. Mr. Hebblethwaite moved on again, and as he went, wondered whether he would not be wise to retire altogether. Joe Puddaby seemed to have disappeared.

While he was hesitating, he noticed that his fellow-guests were nearly all making for a door at the far end of the library, and he heard somebody say something about supper. This stopped his departure at once. It was just after eleven, and he was both hungry and thirsty. Moreover, there was no sense in attending a reception in high society if he failed to discover how and what high society ate and drank. No Yorkshireman could have left at such a moment. So Mr. Hebblethwaite went with the glittering tide, which swept through the door from the library, down some stairs, and into a long room nobly enriched with food and drink and attendant waiters.

"Champagne, sir?" inquired a waiter.

Mr. Hebblethwaite said he would. There were a great many curious and delectable things to eat, and Mr. Hebblethwaite, who had a large appetite, a sound digestion, and an interest in everything that was rich and strange, helped himself liberally. So did most of his fellow-guests. Mr. Hebblethwaite had always imagined that in high society you only trifled in a languid fashion with food and drink, but he soon saw that he had been mistaken. He noticed that elderly woman with the hollow rouged cheeks and the tremendous curved nose, the woman who had mistaken him for someone else. She was gobbling away furiously, like a ravenous old bird. "And I'd rather keep you a week than a fortnight," Mr. Hebblethwaite told her, under his breath.

He felt much better, more at home, now. He attributed this to the food. The fact that he drank, rather quickly, several glasses of champagne did not worry him at all. The crowded rooms had been hot and had made him thirsty, and the food was of a kind that only increased one's thirst. The champagne was beautifully cold and sparkling, and he drank it as if it were mere lemonade. The result was that everything looked bigger and brighter and Mr. Hebblethwaite began to feel at home, no longer a dubious stranger, an uninvited guest, a crasher of gates. A new sense of well-being invaded him. He was at peace with the world, even this world of titles and diamonds and rouge and stars and ribbons. They were really not bad folk at all, when you came to have a good look at them.

He, Tom Hebblethwaite, was a good fellow, a lucky fellow, too. If the large man with the soldierly moustache had turned up, Mr. Hebblethwaite was convinced that the two of them might have had a friendly talk. Such was his new mood. And it was at this moment that his adventures really began, that Lady Gairloch's reception suddenly took a queer turn and became an Arabian Nights entertainment with the result that Mr. Hebblethwaite had a story to tell that his Ludden-stall friends never believed.

It happened in this way. Having eaten and drunk to his satisfaction, Mr. Hebblethwaite found himself wanting to smoke, and, seeing several men help themselves to cigars from a number of boxes in a corner of the room, he made his way there, and selected a cigar of moderate size but excellent quality. Having lit this cigar, he was about to leave this corner of the room when he suddenly noticed his hostess, Lady Gair-loch, who was leaning forward, talking earnestly to a lady who was sitting down, facing one of the tables. Among the many articles of jewellery worn by Lady Gairloch was a superb necklace of pearls. And at that moment, Mr. Hebblethwaite saw this necklace slide away from her neck and vanish. It looked like sheer magic, but there it was. Nobody else noticed it. Lady Gairloch herself was busy leaning forward and talking. Her companion was sitting down and looking another way.

Everybody else there was busy eating, drinking, chattering. Mr. Hebblethwaite was sure he was not mistaken. The pearl necklace had just been quietly unfastened at the back and stolen.

He took a quick step or two forward, and was just in time to see a man move away from behind Lady Gairloch. This man bore no resemblance to any image of a jewel thief that had ever entered Mr. Hebblethwaite's mind. He was a little elderly man, with a very large, bald pink head, with bushy, gingerish eyebrows, and some gingerish curls remaining just above his ears. He looked rather like a round pink little animal that had rubbed off most of its fur. But Mr. Hebblethwaite was ready to swear that it was this little oddity who had just taken the necklace.

After moving away from Lady Gairloch, this elderly man stopped and gave a quick, cunning glance round. His eyes met the accusing gaze of Mr. Hebblethwaite, who was staring hard at him. At once his absurd face brightened. He gave Mr. Hebblethwaite a prodigious wink. Then he grinned, turned away, and disappeared into the crowd of eaters and drinkers and chatterers.

Mr. Hebblethwaite went after him. He managed to keep that bobbing pink head more or less in view down the length of the room, and was in time to see it disappear through the doorway. Still puffing away at his cigar, Mr. Hebblethwaite went through the doorway, too, and up the stairs, back into the long library, which was now almost deserted. But the queer little elderly man was there and when he saw Mr. Hebblethwaite he waved a hand—as if they were playing a little game together—and trotted off again. He opened a door between two great cases of books, a door that Mr. Hebblethwaite had not noticed before, and vanished behind it. Mr. Hebblethwaite, fired now by the heat of the chase, did not stop to think at all, but followed him, and found himself climbing a short curving flight of stairs that brought him to the door, now standing open, of a cosy little room, obviously used as a small study. In this study, standing before the fire, was the elderly little man.

Mr. Hebblethwaite felt that this was no time to beat about the bush. "Look here," he began, abruptly, "I saw you take that necklace downstairs."

"You didn't," said the little elderly man, peevishly.

"I did," said Mr. Hebblethwaite.

"Then you've got a pair of very sharp eyes," the other remarked, still in an absurd, peevish tone. "And why the devil a fellow with spectacles should have a pair of very sharp eyes, I don't know. Nor does anyone else."

"You admit you took it," said Mr. Hebblethwaite, accusingly.

"I do, but only to prevent an argument. I hate argument. Talk, talk, talk, talk, talk," cried the queer little man, "and what good does it do anybody? Of course I took it, and you must agree with me that it was neat work, devilish neat. Wasn't it now?" He put his head slightly on one side as he said this, and looked rather wistful.

"Oh, I don't say it were badly done," Mr. Hebblethwaite admitted. "And I doubt if I'd ha' noticed it at all if I hadn't just been looking that way."

"Well spoken!" The little man held out his hand. "I like the look of you. What's your name?"

Mr. Hebblethwaite told him.

"A damned odd name, too, if you don't mind my saying so," the little man continued. "But you're no worse for that, not a bit the worse. And I like the look of you. Well, you want to see that necklace, I suppose." With this he plunged his right hand into his left inside pocket and then his left tail pocket, and then searched his right inside pocket and tail pocket with his left hand. The result was astounding. On to a little table he poured a glittering heap of jewellery. There was the pearl necklace and several other necklaces, some bracelets, two watches, and some other miscellaneous articles of adornment that Mr. Hebblethwaite had not time to examine.

"By gow!" cried Mr. Hebblethwaite, staring at this heap of gold and platinum and precious stones. "You've had a good haul, haven't you?"

The queer little man chuckled. "Neat work, y'know, very neat work, Mr. Pebblebait," he exclaimed, with satisfaction. Then he leaned forward, confidentially. "Mind you, I don't say I haven't done better. I've done much better, much, much better. But this isn't bad, is it?" He ran his fingers caressingly through the heap of jewellery. Then he stopped, and looked very cunning. "Wait a minute, though. This won't do. We can't stand here like this, looking at these things. We ought to be disguised. I've got them somewhere." He began ransacking his pockets again, and this time produced two false beards and several chocolates. "You see the idea," he went on very solemnly. "We've got to wear these if we're going to look at this stuff." And without more ado, he put on a very unconvincing gingerish beard, turning himself into a still more fantastic personage, and held out the other, a pointed black affair, to his companion. "Put this on at once," he commanded.

The evening had now got out of hand altogether and was taking on the quality of a monstrous dream. But Mr. Hebblethwaite still had some wits left, and these implored him not to don that ridiculous beard. He realised, too, that he had to do with a sort of harmless elderly lunatic, whose hobby it was, apparently, to steal jewellery, or perhaps only to pretend to steal it. Obviously, from his knowledge of the house and the way in which he coolly left the library and came up to this private room, he was either a relative or friend of the family. Meanwhile, as these thoughts passed through his mind, he did not make any attempt to put on the beard.

This annoyed the little man. "Put it on," he cried, his voice rising almost to a shriek. "Put it on, I tell you. We've got to be prepared for anything. What do you think I have these disguises for? Put it on."

To humour him for a minute or two, Mr. Hebblethwaite slipped the beard on. It hooked on to his ears quite snugly. And the sight of it there pleased the little man enormously.

"That's better," he cried. "Now we'll look over this stuff, though I can tell you now that it's not what I expected. Helen's parties are evidently not what they were. Have a chocolate."

"Nay, I've had enough to-night without starting on chocolates," said Mr. Hebblethwaite, from behind his beard.

"It seems to me, Pebblebait," said the little man, severely, "you don't know how to enjoy life. You haven't the technique. Now I"—and here he picked up a chocolate and crunched it solemnly—"like to enjoy myself. But then, I'm an older man than you are, and I know more about the world. That's true, isn't it? I should think it is—devilish true."

At this moment, a telephone buzzed at Mr. Hepplethwaite's elbow. His companion rushed across and at once picked up the receiver. "What's that?" he cried impatiently. "Oh yes, he is. He's speaking now. Yes. Must I? All right then; if I must,

I will." He put down the receiver and looked at Mr. Hebblethwaite, whom he appeared to regard now as his confederate in some vast criminal scheme. "I'm wanted below," he said. "No, don't move. I'll be back in a minute or two."

"But I'm not going to stop here," Mr. Hebblethwaite protested.

"You are. You must, or there'll be the devil to pay. Keep your eye on these trinkets. And have a chocolate. You must have a chocolate. I shan't be long."

He went out, still wearing his false beard. Mr. Hebblethwaite, also still wearing his false beard, was left alone in a strange room in a strange house, with a good many thousand pounds' worth of jewellery on the table in front of him. It seemed to him absurd to remain where he was. Obviously, the best thing to do was to take off this daft beard, creep downstairs and clear out of the house, leaving Lady Gairloch to discover her necklace for herself. But no sooner had he decided to go than quick footsteps sounded up the stairs outside, the door was flung open, and in came a most monstrous and unexpected figure. He was one of the enormous footmen that Mr. Hebblethwaite had seen in the great hall below. Mr. Hebblethwaite recognised him by his light blue footman's livery. But that is all that he could recognise, for this footman was wearing a black mask. Mr. Hebblethwaite stared open-mouthed at this apparition. The man might have come straight from a fancy-dress ball or the last scene in some light opera.

"Stay where you are, buddy," said this masked footman, advancing with a revolver in one hand. "Don't move. I'm here on business. I'm not playing hunt-the-thimble, don't make any mistake about that."

"What's the idea?" cried Mr. Hebblethwaite.

"Ah, there they are. I thought his lordship would bring his little packet up here with him. Very nice too, very nice! Stand further back, you. Go on, stand further back. The necklace, too. Oh, very nice, couldn't be nicer. Here, I'll take this lot, and you can have the rest, Rasputin. Fine!"

He grabbed the necklace and one or two of the other things, turned away and made for the door. Maddened by the cool audacity of this raid, Mr. Hebblethwaite sprang forward ready to risk the revolver. Evidently, the man had no intention of offering violence, clearly preferring to get away as soon as possible without making a noise. Mr. Hebblethwaite's hand touched the back of his coat, but that is all. The man gave one bound and was outside the room, and Mr. Hebblethwaite found the door slammed in his face, and not only slammed but locked. The man had taken the precaution of removing the key from the inside when he first entered, and now Mr. Hebblethwaite was locked in and was wasting a little precious time in rattling the handle.

"By gow, he did it on me right that time," he told himself, turning away from the stubborn door. What was to be done now? Should he use the telephone, and let them—whoever the mysterious "them" might be—know all that he himself knew? Or should he wait until the queer little elderly man— evidently Lord Somebody-or-other—returned, as he had promised to do? Though it was probably ridiculous to take any notice of his eccentric lordship's promises, for the pink little man was as mad as a hatter. Pondering these things, Mr. Hebblethwaite went back to the table and involuntarily his hand strayed to the remaining baubles. He felt far less giddy and exhilarated now than he had felt when he had first gone in pursuit of his kleptomaniacal lordship, but that does not mean that he felt any better. On the contrary, he felt worse. Things were still misty but were no longer pleasant. The sense of well-being had departed, with the ebb of that golden tide of champagne. He had a slight headache. He sat down, with the jewellery he had been playing with still in his hands. But he was not thinking about it. He was wondering what to do next.

What he did do next was to stare very uncomfortably at his next visitor, who stood in the doorway, surveying him, with a triumphant gleam in his eye and a contemptuous smile so broad that it could easily be seen behind the soldierly moustache. Yes, it was the large suspicious man with the soldierly moustache. The sight of Mr. Hebblethwaite appeared to give him great entertainment

"Well, well, well!" he cried. "So here we are, nicely locked in, too. And here's some of the stuff, too, all ready to hand. Well, well, well! I'll say this for you—you're very clever up to a point, very clever. But like a lot of 'em, you don't take long reaching the point. Well, take the whiskers off. This isn't a children's party."

Mr. Hebblethwaite then realised, with considerable annoyance, that he was still wearing that beard, and he took the thing off and flung it on the floor. "I'd forgotten about that daft thing," he cried.

"There are several things you've forgotten, my friend," said his visitor.

"Now listen here," cried Mr. Hebblethwaite, "I can see you're beginning to fancy yourself because you think you've made a great catch. But you're making a big mistake."

"Of course I am," said the detective, with tremendous irony. "When I asked you your name, downstairs, you gave me a name that isn't on the list of guests. My mistake, of course. Then I find you up here, in a part of the house that's private, and here you are, with a false beard on, and you're holding some stolen jewellery in your hand. My mistake, of course. You just happened to come to the party without being invited, didn't you? And you're just sitting up here to cool off a bit, aren't you? And you're wearing a false beard because you've got into the habit of wearing one at this time of night, keeps your chin warm—aren't you? And you don't know anything about those articles you're holding in your hand, do you? Oh no." And the detective gave a very hollow laugh.

Mr. Hebblethwaite realised that he must appear the most suspicious of suspicious characters. Indeed, with such a case against him, he actually felt rather guilty. This man with the soldierly moustache—and really, when you came to think of it, he had "detective" written all over him—seemed to have been making him feel guilty half the night.

"Well?"

"As a matter of fact, what you've just said—about why I happened to be here and all that—is about right, near enough, any road. And it's a fact I don't know anything about these things i' my hand. They were left here by somebody else, if you want to know."

"Go hon," said the detective, smiling ironically.

"If you think I'm a crook like, what i' the name o' wonder d'you think I'd be sitting here for?" Mr. Hebblethwaite demanded, with some heat. "And another thing. Seeing you're so clever, you might explain how I come to lock myself in here. You must ha' noticed t'door were locked, 'cos you unlocked it."

Obviously this puzzled the detective, who began rubbing his chin. "Look here, let's have your story."

Mr. Hebblethwaite told his story, beginning with his acceptance of another man's invitation card and going on to his acquaintance with the queer little elderly man.

Here the detective broke in. "Ah, that's her ladyship's uncle, Lord Hornyhold. Bit off his head, of course. He's famous for taking things. Doesn't want 'em, y'know, but enjoys himself taking 'em. So you followed him up here?"

"I did, and this is part of his night's catch," said Mr. Hebblethwaite, "but the best lot's gone, and it's going now while we're talking." And hastily he plunged into an account of the visit of the masked footman.

"Now that's serious," cried the detective. "That's just what I'm here to prevent. There are twelve of these chaps, and four of 'em are new, taken on for these affairs. A clever crook could easily work it that way. And all the same size and in the same uniform, and this chap was masked. You wouldn't know him again, would you? That is, even if he's here to know, though for that matter, if he's clever he will be."

"I'll have a shot at telling him again," said Mr. Hebblethwaite with determination. "Don't say nowt but just let me have a squint at these footmen chaps, and I'll see. And take this stuff. I don't want it." He handed over the jewellery.

"But don't try anything on, you know," said the detective, in a warning tone. "I haven't seen this crook footman of yours yet, don't forget."

They went quickly downstairs, to the hall, and there found eight out of the twelve footmen. Saying nothing, Mr. Hebblethwaite walked swiftly round them all, and then took the detective on one side. "You see that one there, him by the statue. That's him. Get that butler chap to ask him to come into a little room somewhere and then we'll see if I'm not right."

The detective took the butler on one side and whispered to him, and the butler gave the footman in question an order to wait upon two gentlemen in one of the small ante-rooms. The two gentlemen were there, waiting for him, and both gentlemen grabbed an arm when he made an appearance.

"I've got him," cried Mr. Hebblethwaite. "Now you turn his pockets out."

The detective may have had his weaknesses but he was certainly good at turning pockets out, and in less than a minute he was holding up Lady Gairloch's necklace and the other missing things. There was no revolver, and evidently the man had thought it safer to get rid of that. It was not long before he was removed to a safe place.

"One of the new lot," the detective explained, "but a proper crook, of course, and clever, too. I believe I've seen him before. But how did you manage to recognise him?"

"Ay, well, we're not all so silly as we look." Mr. Hebblethwaite observed. "But if you want to know, I'll tell you. I just got my hand to his back before he got to t'door upstairs, and I happened to have a bit o' chocolate in my hand and it daubed his coat, and being a light blue coat it showed. Nobody could ha' noticed it if they weren't looking for it, but I knew what I were looking for and when I walked round 'em I found it all right."

"Smart work. And I don't mind telling you, you've got me out of a devil of a mess. Her ladyship had missed that necklace all right, but she thought her uncle had it, and the other things as well. It was the queer fellow, y'know, who rang up his lordship in the study on the chance of his leaving the stuff behind him. He must have been watching him when he was on duty in the supper-room. But look here, you've done me a good turn, and if you like, I'll take you to her ladyship now and tell her the whole story and show her what you did."

"No fear," cried Mr. Hebblethwaite. "If you want to do me a good turn, get me my hat and coat and let me get out o' this, and when I'm out, keep me out of it. I've had enough o' this high society. It's nowt i' my line."

"Suits me all right," said the detective.

"Well, then, we're both suited," said Mr. Hebblethwaite, not realising that nobody now would believe his Arabian Nights adventure in Park Lane. "Let me get out quietly and off home to bed."

THE TAXI AND THE STAR

Mr. Hebblethwaite, buyer for the Luddenstall Cooperative Society, was in a desperate hurry, so desperate a hurry that he decided to take a taxi. When a man from Luddenstall, or from any similar place in the West Riding, is willing to take a taxi, though not encumbered with any luggage or on his way to catch a train, you may be sure that desperation has set in, for Luddenstall looks queerly at any man who is ready to take taxis as if they were buses or trams. Heads are shaken over such men, and afterwards, when the inevitable crash arrives, it is pointed out that "they couldn't carry corn." Now Mr. Hebblethwaite, as anybody in Luddenstall would admit, was a man who *could* carry corn. If he demanded a taxi, then you may be sure that the situation urgently demanded a taxi too. And so it did, for Mr. Hebblethwaite had only eight minutes in which to catch Mr. Greenbaum, of Huskins and Greenbaum, wholesale millinery. Mr. Greenbaum was to be found in Aldersgate Street, whereas Mr. Hebblethwaite was standing in the upper part of Shaftesbury Avenue.

It was one of those miserable, wet afternoons when nearly all the London taxi-drivers, who wait and wait for custom on fine days, seem to sneak off home to their startled wives. For a minute or two there was not a single empty taxi to be seen. Mr. Hebblethwaite, standing at the kerb, shouted to two or three, but they were all engaged; and there is something even more humiliating about making advances to engaged taxis than there is about making advances to engaged girls. As they went splashing past, these taxis seemed to sneer. Mr. Hebblethwaite, who felt that he had shown great enterprise by deciding to take a taxi at all, was annoyed. Where, now, were all those waiting cabs he noticed every time he came to London?

At last one came crawling along, looking hungry. Mr. Hebblethwaite shouted to it and waved his hand. It heard him and saw him, and approached. But when it was just slowing up, a shortish man, with a large head and a hat too small for him, popped up from nowhere and promptly stepped in front of Mr. Hebblethwaite.

"That's right," he said to the driver. "Here you are."

"Here, half a minute," said Mr. Hebblethwaite. "This taxi came for me, not you."

"Oh, no! Oh no! My taxi," the man replied, with an autocratic wave of his hand. He seemed to be quite an autocratic little man. Now he addressed the driver. "You came for me, didn't you? You know me—Victor Cranton—don't you? Course you do. I waved to you first."

"That's right, sir," said the driver, with a grin, and held the door open for him. And before Mr. Hebblethwaite could do anything beyond making preliminary noises of protest, this

Victor Cranton had shouted the address he wanted, slipped into the cab, and had departed, leaving Mr. Hebblethwaite still waiting in the rain, very angry.

He considered that a very dirty little trick had been played upon him, and though the taxi-driver was partly responsible, the real instigator of it was Mr. Victor Cranton, shortish, with a large head, and a hat too small for him. The name seemed vaguely familiar. Mr. Hebblethwaite, belatedly on his way to Huskins and Greenbaum, brooded over this name, its owner, and the trick he had been served. "An' if ivver I've a chance, lad," he told a mental image of Mr. Cranton, "I'll get one back on you."

Such a chance appeared to be very remote, yet, so curiously twisted are the strands of this life, an opportunity arrived during Mr. Hebblethwaite's very next visit to London. On the very first night of his visit he left his modest little hotel in Bloomsbury for a magnificent and horribly expensive service flat in Mayfair. The owner of this flat was a colossal celebrity, a woman whose name and face were known throughout England and the Eastern States of America. And yet, when Mr. Hebblethwaite walked in, this delicious and famous creature immediately rushed up to him and at once imprinted a large and luscious kiss on his cheek, a kiss that he received quite calmly.

However much we may prefer short and dramatic methods, it is obvious that we must depart from them for a moment here. That visit and that kiss demand an immediate explanation. The fact is that Mr. Hebblethwaite was only incidentally visiting Miss Allie Marsden, the famous music-hall and revue star. The person he was really visiting was Alice Marsden, who was Mrs. Hebblethwaite's cousin and a Luddenstall lass. Alice Marsden went on the stage and became Allie Marsden, and, after a few years of very hard work and very little money, suddenly caught the fancy of West End audiences with the very same tricks of voice and gesture that had made Luddenstall laugh years before. After that, Allie worked up a tremendous career for herself, on the halls, in revue, and in films. She was not pretty, and her rather short, square figure could not be called beautiful; but she had a stage personality as vivid as a flash of lightning, any amount of charm when she wanted it, a little trick of pathos, and a whole Pennine range of North-country humour. She never received less than four hundred pounds for a week's work, and there was not a box-office manager in London or New York who would have denied that she was worth every penny of it. Actually, she was now neither Alice Marsden of Luddenstall nor Miss Allie Marsden of the bills, but Mrs. Richard Haycroft, wife of a stalwart and good-looking stockbroker.

"Well, Tom, lad," cried the famous person, dropping back again into the Luddenstall tongue, "it's nice to see you. Get yourself a drink. Dick'll be in, in a minute. How's Rose?" Rose was her cousin, now Mrs. Hebblethwaite.

"She's champion," said Mr. Hebblethwaite. "And so's the family."

"That's grand. I'd like to see 'em again. Why don't you bring 'em all up here to see me, Tom?"

"Why don't you come an' see us, Allie?" Mr. Hebblethwaite retorted. "It's easier. There's fewer of you, and more brass to do it on."

In Luddenstall, the rule in conversation is candour, and the great Allie was not at all offended by these remarks.

"I've been thinking," she said seriously, "I'd like to have a look at t'owd shop again, Tom. But I don't know when I can manage it. I've just come back from America specially for this new show here, *Ducks and Drakes*."

"I know that, lass," said Mr. Hepplethwaite. "We read all about it i' t'paper. We can't pick up a paper without there's summat about you. We're getting fair sick an' tired o' hearing tell of you, Allie. I met owd Joe Holmes t'other day—you remember him?"

"Think I do!" cried the celebrity, her face lighting up. "He once chased me out of his shop."

"Well, an' I'll bet you asked fo' it an' all. You wor a cheeky kid. But I met owd Joe t'other day, an' he says, 'They mun be fast what to put in t'paper these days when they can print so much silly stuff about Jack Marsden's lass. You might think she wor t'Queen o' England, t'way they go on abaht her.' So you see, Allie."

She laughed at this. "I must see old Joe again, Tom. Perhaps if I put my tongue out at him, he'd chase me out of his shop again. You know, Tom, I work very hard nowadays and I've a lot of responsibility, but I have a good time——"

"An' I should think an' all. If you don't, who does?"

"I'll tell you one who does, Tom. That's Rose. Oh yes, I know what you're going to say. But Rose has got all she wants—she's got you and those three grand little kids—and she's happy. I know that. And I'm glad. But what I was going to say was this: I have a good time, in spite of the hard work and the responsibility and the nerves and the palaver—but I often think I'd like to be a kid again, walking down Moor Lane with a dirty little red tam-o'-shanter at the back of my head and a big hole in my stocking. That's when you have the fun, lad. It's not the same when you get older, they can say what they like. Perhaps it'ud be different if I'd some kids of my own, just to watch them."

"Aye, it makes a difference," said Mr. Hebblethwaite awkwardly, not at his ease with her in this rare sentimental mood.

"But as I was saying," she continued, more briskly, "I can't manage a trip up North. I've been hard at it rehearsing ever since I came back. I only just knocked off an hour ago. They're still at it now, but I said, 'Here, I've had enough for to-day,' and walked out. I'm tired, lad, I can tell you. Talk about the Luddenstall Co-op. It's a picnic compared to my job."

"And paid accordingly," said Mr. Hebblethwaite, dryly. "Hello, here's Dick."

"Hello, Tom! What about a little drink? Had one, Allie?" Dick Haycroft helped himself, then beamed upon the other two. "What's the news from Luddenstall, Tom? How's trade?"

"Well, it's a bit better than it was," said Mr. Hebblethwaite, cautiously. And for the next five minutes he and Dick discussed trade in general.

"How did the *Ducks and Drakes* go to-day, Allie?" asked her husband. "I saw your musical chap—what's his name?— Akeley—at the club to-night, for a minute, and he said they were all quacking in pretty good style."

"I was just telling Tom," said Allie, "I walked out on 'em about an hour ago. I'd had enough for one day."

"Quite right."

"I'm getting a bit fed up with Victor," Allie continued. "His head's swelling. And just because I know how difficult it all is and try to play fair and don't give him the temperamental star stuff, he's beginning to think I'll eat out of his hand. He's done so well lately that it's going to be hard for him to get his head down Shaftesbury Avenue. They'll have to widen it for him."

"And who's this Victor when he's at home?" Mr. Hebblethwaite inquired. His acquaintance with the theatrical world was limited to Allie.

"That's a good one, Allie," cried her husband. "We ought to tell Victor that one. That'll larn him. Who is he? Ha, ha!"

"I'll bet anything he comes round to-night," said Allie, screwing up her delightful features in a manner familiar to so many audiences: "Just for two minutes, my dear—only two-oo-oo minutes. Busiest man in London, my dear."

"Victor to the life!" And Dick applauded.

"Must run away after two-oo-oo minutes. Haven't had a moment to myself, my dear, since last July. The great Victor Cranton."

"Is that his name?" cried Mr. Hebblethwaite.

"Of course, it is, Tom lad. And don't start pretending you've never heard of it before. I don't mind you doing so to him—it'll do him good—but don't try it on with me. Victor Cranton's one of our biggest men in the theatre now, and he's recently engaged me—which was very sensible of him—to play in his new show, *Ducks and Drakes*."

"She's the chief Doock," said Dick, having a shot—for the millionth time—at a north-country accent, and missing it.

"I've heard of him all right," said Mr. Hebblethwaite, grimly. "But I didn't know what he was. Here—is he a shortish chap with a big head and a hat too small for him?"

"Sounds like him," Allie replied. "I don't suppose he could get a hat big enough for him now; they wouldn't sell one big enough for the new head he's getting. But I'm tired of Victor. Let's talk about something else. What's happening at the Moor Lane Congregational Chapel these days?"

Her husband laughed.

"Don't laugh, yer gurt nowt," cried Allie. "I used to go to the Moor Lane Congs., didn't I, Tom? When I was sixteen, I tried to get into the choir—as a so-prano—do, mee, so, der-ho—but old Halstead wouldn't have me in. Tom was in, among the basses—weren't you, Tom? But Tom was grown up then, with a moustache too. He was rather good-looking then—don't blush, Tom; you were, but that's a long time since—and we used to make eyes at him and gather round him at the bazaars, but our Rose got in first, because she was the nicest and prettiest. D'you remember, Tom? Dick, shut up. We want to have a serious Luddenstall conversation, don't we, Tom? If you don't keep quiet, Dick, I'll go to Luddenstall tomorrow morning."

Mr. Victor Cranton did visit them that night. He arrived about an hour later, and, as Allie had prophesied, he announced at once that he could only stay for two minutes. On being introduced to Mr. Hebblethwaite, he gave him a nod and then took no further notice of him. With Dick he exchanged about ten words, and accepted a drink from his hands. Then he addressed himself to Allie: "My dear, I can't stay. Only came round for two minutes. I've left Robertson working with the chorus and Jimmy Dudley. But what made you cut away? Of course, it's all right, it's perfectly all right. Only I like to be asked. It's a rule I've made. Everybody at rehearsals, and nobody to leave without my permission—and everybody includes the stars, even *you*, my dear. It's the only way to do it. You remember I signed up Stella Fragerson for my last show, *The Golden Garter*—and then she never appeared? Well, my dear Allie, I'll tell you what happened—in confidence, of course. She wouldn't work my way. I told her—I told her straight. She said, 'I'm Stella Fragerson.' I said, 'And I'm Victor Cranton, and this

is a Victor Cranton production. Now what about it, Stella?'
She threatened to walk out. I called her bluff. She walked.
Well, of course, my dear, you're *not* Stella Fragerson——"

"Thank Heaven!" murmured Dick.

"But that's my way. The public wants a big Victor Cranton
show—they're ready to eat it—and the only way I can give it
to them is to have everybody, *everybody*, working to my plan.
And you know what the results are? Wonderful, my dear,
wonderful—you know that. And now I must run. No, no, old
man, no more—I only slipped in for two minutes, just to have
a word with Allie. Well, see you at eleven to-morrow morning,
my dear."

"You might," said Allie, smiling mysteriously.

He wagged a forefinger at her. "Now, now, Allie. No
teasing. And remember, I may be a bit of an autocrat, but I do
get results. There's no bungling, no mess. Well, I'll run."

"How's that for a head?" Allie asked, when he had gone.

"That's him," Mr. Hebblethwaite announced emphati-
cally. "No mistake about it. That's him."

"Hello, Tom!" cried Allie. "You sound as if you've met
Victor before. He didn't seem to recognise you."

"He didn't. But I recognised him all right. Last time I was
here, that chap played a dirty little trick on me—at least, I
call it a dirty trick. I'll tell you." And he told them the story
of the taxi.

"Now, that's just like him," cried Allie, when the story was
told. "I feel like paying him out for that."

"I've felt that way for some time," said Mr. Hebblethwaite.

"Listen." And Allie put a hand on each man's coat, and
immediately all three of them had a conspiratorial air. "Can't
we do something? Wait a minute. What about this?"

We now present Mr. Victor Cranton on the telephone next

day. "Yes, yes, that's Mrs. Haycroft's house, isn't it? Can I speak to her? Mr. Cranton, Mr. Victor Cranton. It's very urgent. *Ur-gent*, I said. She *must* speak to me. Yes, of course. I'll wait. But hurry up. I say—*hurry up*. Hello! Hel-*lo*! No, I haven't finished. Leave us alone. Hello! Oh, is that you, Allie? Look here, my dear, what *is* the idea? You're going to—*what*? But you can't. You're crazy, my dear. Look here, have a rest to-day and to-morrow. I understand—you're tired, that's what it is, Allie. You want a rest. I've been working you too hard. What's that? You *can't* do that. Oh, you know what I mean. Of course you can if you want to, but look what it means. You'll ruin the whole show. Oh no, Allie, you wouldn't do that. You're joking, my dear. You can't mean it. Look here, I'm coming round to see you. You *must* see me. Just two-oo-oo minutes."

A further scene, very short and dramatic, showing a distracted Mr. Victor Cranton, arriving at the flat of Miss Allie Marsden, and being told very firmly by a maid that she cannot be seen, and told not once but half a dozen times. Exit Mr. Cranton, in smoke and flame.

We now present Mr. Victor Cranton once more on the telephone. It is the day following that on which he made his unsuccessful attempt to see his leading lady. This time he is speaking to her husband. "Look here, Haycroft, old man, I had to ring you. About Allie. Yes, about Allie. I can't get a word out of her, can't see her, can't speak to her. What does it mean? *Wha-a-at?* To where? Luddenstall? What's she want to go there for? Oh, but she's crazy. We're opening next week. I say—*we're opening*. She'll ruin me. She'll ruin herself. She'll ruin all of us. It's suicide. It's murder. But I tell you, something *must* be done. Can't you persuade her? Come along, old man, I'm sure you can. You can't? Who? Who's he? Her cousin? I see. She's going to stay there. What's the name?

Spell it. H-e-b-b-l-e-t-h-w-a-i-t-e. Yes, I've got it. Where's he staying? I see. All right, old man, I'll get hold of him. Good Lord, yes!—I'll work it somehow. Thanks for the tip."

A very obscure provincial person called Hebblethwaite, staying in a rather cheap Bloomsbury hotel, now suddenly became the most important person in London to the great Victor Cranton. This Hebblethwaite was telephoned to, but could not be found. A letter was sent through the post, and then another letter was sent by messenger. Finally, Mr. Cranton himself descended upon the Bloomsbury hotel and insisted upon seeing Mr. Hebblethwaite. The interview took place, at Mr. Hebblethwaite's request, in a very small and very cold bedroom, the kind of place Mr. Cranton had not seen for years. Mr. Hebblethwaite was a very difficult man, for he would not go out and have a meal, or even a drink, with Mr. Cranton. He insisted upon staying in his cold little bedroom. Victor Cranton found it hard to be charming, faced with such a man and such an apartment, but he did his best.

"I don't think you quite realise, Mr. Hebblethwaite," he said earnestly, "what this means to me and to the people who are backing me. Miss Allie Marsden, as you know, is our star. I don't say she's the whole show, by any means; but she's a good part of it, and we can't get on without her. We can't even rehearse properly without her. As for opening without her, it's unthinkable. And every night we delay the opening means a dead loss of several hundred pounds. You're a business man yourself, and you can see what it means."

Mr. Hebblethwaite nodded, but said nothing. He would never have admitted it for the world, but actually this mixture of charm and earnestness was having its effect on him.

"If Miss Marsden was ill, it would be different," Mr. Cranton continued, mournfully now. "We'd have to disappoint the public. There'd be no help for it. But she isn't. It's just a whim. And I didn't expect to be treated like this by Allie Marsden. She's got a name for playing up to her managers and the public, not like some of the stars. She's a Yorkshire girl, and she's always kept her word. Now, look here, Mr. Hebblethwaite. Dick Haycroft tells me that she's going away like this because she wants to stay with you and Mrs. Hebblethwaite at——er—Luddenstall. Very nice. We all like to see the old places again. But you can see yourself that this isn't the time to go away. It's not playing the game. It's taking a holiday not at your own expense but at other people's. Dick Haycroft said you could persuade her to stay on in town. Well, what about it, Mr. Hebblethwaite?"

"Aye, what about it?" the other repeated, his face without expression.

"Well, if you'd do that, you'd find Victor Cranton very grateful," that gentleman continued, persuasively. "Look here, you do that for me, Mr. Hebblethwaite, and you can have a whole row of stalls for the first night of *Ducks and Drakes*. I don't know how the devil I'll manage it—because, let me tell you, Victor Cranton's first nights are big events in this city—but I'll manage it. A whole row of stalls, if you want 'em."

A certain self-assertiveness that had crept back into Mr. Cranton's voice made Mr. Hebblethwaite look grim again. "Nay, you can keep your stalls and first nights. This show o' yours is nowt to me. I wouldn't be paid to see it—t'first night or onny other night."

"What?" Mr. Cranton, was genuinely horrified.

"Why should I? Allie Marsden's been making me laugh for twenty year, long afore, you ever set eyes on her, so there's nowt new about her, and as for t'rest of it, you can keep it."

Mr. Cranton stared at this barbarian in despair. "Well," he said, finally, trying to smile, "perhaps there's something else I can do for you. Er—let me see——"

"I'll tell you summat," said Mr. Hebblethwaite, grimly. "I come up here on business, and I find it a bother getting about. T'last time I were up, when it were raining hard nearly all time, I were in a hurry one afternoon and I couldn't get a taxi. But I found one at finish, and I were just getting into it when a chap slipped in front of me and said it were his, and 'cos t'driver knew this chap's name and knew he were well off, this chap got taxi all right and left me stranded." And Mr. Hebblethwaite stared so hard at his companion when he said this that there could be no doubt who the taxi-stealing chap was.

"My dear fellow, d'you mean to say I did that? I'd no idea. I'm terribly sorry, terribly sorry."

"An' so were I at time," said Mr. Hebblethwaite.

"Look here, Mr. Hebblethwaite, I'd not the least idea I'd offended you in this way. Did you tell Allie this? Ah, you did. Now I begin to see daylight. Mr. Hebblethwaite, I don't know how long you're staying in London, but I promise you shall have a car at your disposal for the rest of the time you're here."

"But I don't want a car at my disposal," said Mr. Hebblethwaite. "It were a taxi you robbed me of, so we'll stick to taxis."

"A taxi, then."

"Nay, not one taxi. You can be diddled out o' one taxi so easy. I've seen that. I'll have five taxis, thank you.

"Five taxis! But what you're going to do with them? You can't ride in five taxis."

Mr. Hebblethwaite grinned. "I'll ride i' t'middle one, and have two in front an' two at back. An' if you see I've got five taxis in t'morning, Mr. Cranton, an' mak' arrangements for me to use 'em as long as I'm here, I promise you'll not have any more bother wi' Miss Allie Marsden."

Mr. Cranton clapped his hands. "Done. It's a bargain. You'll have five taxis in the morning, Mr. Hebblethwaite. They'll be waiting outside this hotel at—er—what time shall we say?—ten o'clock, eh? Right. And now what about getting hold of Allie?"

"Come downstairs and I'll ring her up now an' settle it for you," said Mr. Hebblethwaite, with more than a shade of patronage in his tone. He went first, and he did not see the smile that had now found its way to Mr. Cranton's broad and very intelligent face. If he had seen that smile, he might have felt less triumphant.

After the short and successful telephone conversation with the star, Mr. Hebblethwaite and Mr. Cranton shook hands. "Five taxis, eh?" said the latter, chuckling. "An amusing idea, that. I congratulate you. Well, I must run. I've got an idea, too. Look out for the five taxis in the morning. They'll be outside here."

They were. Mr. Cranton kept his word, and, being a born showman, had turned that word to good account. The publicity agent of *Ducks and Drakes* had had a very busy time since that little talk between Messrs. Hebblethwaite and Cranton. Many strings came easily into that agent's hands, and he had been pulling them hard. That obscure Bloomsbury hotel favoured by Mr. Hebblethwaite had been suddenly put on the map.

Mr. Hebblethwaite came down to find the five taxis awaiting him and a great deal else too. There were six reporters in the hall, all waiting for his "story." There were four ordinary press photographers and two men with film cameras, all waiting for him to climb into the middle taxi and order the cavalcade to start. There were about two hundred idle sightseers waiting too, attracted by the spectacle of the taxis and the camera-men. There were three policemen and a sergeant, keeping the crowd from blocking up the entrance to the hotel. The man from Luddenstall was given a hint as to what the word "publicity" meant in London.

He pushed his way through the little swarm of reporters, who were all asking him questions that he did not answer, and glared at the array of cabs, cameras, policemen, and spectators outside the front door.

"Mr. 'Ebblethwaite, that right?" said a husky voice. It came from the leader of the five taxi-drivers.

"That's right," said Mr. Hebblethwaite. "And I don't want you, any of you. Who d'you think I am? Mary Pickford? I'm not going to mak' a show o' myself. Go on, clear off. I don't want you."

They went, but not before the cameras had clicked and the reporters had made a few mental notes. If Mr. Hebblethwaite imagined that by not using even one of the five taxis he would escape publicity, he was sadly mistaken. Wheels had been set in motion that he could not stop. The camera-men had been sent out to take pictures, and they took them. The reporters had been sent out to get a "story," and they got it. They got little from Mr. Hebblethwaite himself, but they had Victor Cranton's publicity man to fall back upon, and they fell back upon him. Mr. Hebblethwaite was in two of the evening papers that night, and in three of the morning papers the next day, and there were photographs, too. The story the press told was an amusing one, but Victor Cranton seemed to be the hero of it. Mr. Hebblethwaite, the man who had refused to give the journalists the information they required, appeared to play a rather foolish part in it.

"And I don't see," said Mr. Hebblethwaite to Miss Allie Marsden, "that I did get even wi' yond chap Cranton. He'd got t'laugh at me at finish."

"Well, I will say that for Victor," replied the star, "He's bossy, but he's clever. But if I do come to Luddenstall, Tom, I won't say nowt about it."

"Nay, lass, it doesn't matter," said Mr. Hebblethwaite, who knew his Luddenstall.

"You can bet your boots they know now."

THE DEMON KING

Among the company assembled for Mr. Tom Burt's Grand Annual Pantomime at the old Theatre Royal, Bruddersford, there was a good deal of disagreement. They were not quite "the jolly, friendly party" they pretended to be—through the good offices of "Thespian"—to the readers of *The Bruddersford Herald* and *Weekly Herald Budget*. The Principal Boy told her husband and about fifty-five other people that she could work with anybody, was famous for being able to work with anybody, but that nevertheless the management had gone and engaged, as Principal Girl, the one woman in the profession who made it almost impossible for anybody to work with anybody. The Principal Girl told her friend, the Second Boy, that the Principal Boy and the Second Girl were spoiling everything and might easily ruin the show. The Fairy Queen went about pointing out that she did not want to make trouble, being notoriously easy-going, but that sooner or later the Second Girl would hear a few things that she would not like. Johnny Wingfield had been heard to declare that some people did not realise even yet that what audiences wanted from a panto was some good fast comedy work by the chief comedian, who had to have all the scope he required. Dippy and Doppy, the broker's men, hinted that even if there were two stages, Johnny Wingfield would want them both all the time.

But they were all agreed on one point, namely, that there was not a better demon in provincial panto than Mr. Kirk Ireton, who had been engaged by Mr. Tom Burt for this particular show. The pantomime was *Jack and Jill*, and those people who are puzzled to know what demons have to do with Jack and Jill, those innocent water-fetchers, should pay a visit to the nearest pantomime, which will teach them a lot they did not know about fairy tales. Kirk Ireton was not merely a demon, but the Demon King, and when the curtain first went up, you saw him on a darkened stage standing in front of a little chorus of attendant demons, made up of local baritones at ten shillings a night. Ireton looked the part, for he was tall and rather satanically featured and was known to be very clever with his make-up; and what was more important, he sounded the part too, for he had a tremendous bass voice, of most demonish quality. He had played Mephistopheles in *Faust* many times with a good touring opera company. He was, indeed, a man with a fine future behind him. If it had not been for one weakness, pantomime would never have seen him. The trouble was that for years now he had been in the habit of "lifting the elbow" too much. That was how they all put it. Nobody said that he drank too much, but all agreed that he lifted the elbow. And the problem now was—would there be trouble because of his elbow-lifting?

He had rehearsed with enthusiasm, sending his great voice to the back of the empty, forlorn gallery in the two numbers allotted to him, but at the later rehearsals there had been ominous signs of elbow-lifting.

"Going to be all right, Mr. Ireton?" the stage-manager inquired anxiously.

Ireton raised his formidable and satanic eyebrows. "Of course it is," he replied, somewhat hoarsely. "What's worrying you, old man?"

The other explained hastily that he wasn't worried. "You'll go well here" he went on. "They'll eat those two numbers of yours. Very musical in these parts. But you know Bruddersford of course. You've played here before."

"I have," replied Ireton, grimly. "And I loathe the dam' place. Bores me stiff. Nothing to do in it."

This was not reassuring. The stage-manager knew only too well Mr. Ireton was already finding something to do in the town, and his enthusiastic description of the local golf courses had no effect. Ireton loathed golf too, it seemed. All very ominous.

They were opening on Boxing Day night. By the afternoon it was known that Kirk Ireton had been observed lifting the elbow very determinedly in the smoke-room of "The Cooper's Arms," near the theatre. One of the stage hands had seen him: "And by gow, he wor lapping it up an' all," said this gentleman, no bad judge of anybody's power of suction. From there, it appeared, he had vanished, along with several other riotous persons, two of them thought to be Leeds men—and in Bruddersford they know what Leeds men are.

The curtain was due to rise at seven-fifteen sharp. Most members of the company arrived at the theatre very early. Kirk Ireton was not one of them. He was still absent at six-thirty, though he had to wear an elaborate make-up, with glittering tinselled eyelids and all the rest of it, and had to be on the stage when the curtain rose. A messenger was dispatched to his lodgings, which were not far from the theatre. Even before the messenger returned, to say that Mr. Ireton had not been in since noon, the stage-manager was desperately coaching one of the local baritones, the best of a stiff and stupid lot, in the part of the Demon King. At six forty-five, no Ireton; at seven, no Ireton. It was hopeless.

"All right, that fellow's done for himself now," said the great Mr. Burt, who had come to give his Grand Annual his blessing. "He doesn't get another engagement from me as long as he lives. What's this local chap like?"

The stage-manager groaned and wiped his brow. "Like nothing on earth except a bow-legged baritone from a Wesleyan choir."

"He'll have to manage somehow. You'll have to cut the part."

"Cut it, Mr. Burt! I've slaughtered it, and what's left of it, he'll slaughter."

Mr. Tom Burt, like the sensible manager he was, believed in a pantomime opening in the old-fashioned way, with a mysterious dark scene among the supernaturals. Here it was a cavern in the hill beneath the Magic Well, and in these dismal recesses the Demon King and his attendants were to be discovered waving their crimson cloaks and plotting evil in good, round chest-notes. Then the Demon King would sing his number (which had nothing whatever to do with Jack and Jill or demonology either), the Fairy Queen would appear, accompanied by a white spotlight, there would be a little dialogue between them, and then a short duet.

The cavern scene was all set, the five attendant demons were in their places, while the sixth, now acting as King, was receiving a few last instructions from the stage-manager, and the orchestra, beyond the curtain, were coming to the end of the overture, when suddenly, from nowhere, there appeared on the dimly-lighted stage a tall and terrifically imposing figure.

"My God! There's Ireton," cried the stage-manager, and bustled across, leaving the temporary Demon King, abandoned, a pitiful makeshift now. The new arrival was coolly taking his place in the centre. He looked superb. The costume, a skin-tight crimson affair touched with a baleful green, was far better than the one provided by the management. And the make-up was better still. The face had a greenish phosphorescent glow, and its eyes flashed between glittering lids. When he first caught sight of that face, the stage-manager felt a sudden idiotic tremor of fear, but being a stage-manager first and a human being afterwards (as all stage-managers have to be), he did not feel that tremor long, for it was soon chased away by a sense of elation. It flashed across his mind that Ireton must have gone running off to Leeds or somewhere in search of this stupendous costume and make-up. Good old Ireton! He had given them all a fright, but it had been worth it.

"All right, Ireton?" said the stage-manager, quickly.

"All right," replied the Demon King, with a magnificent careless gesture.

"Well, you get back in the chorus then," said the stage-manager to the Wesleyan baritone.

"That'll do me champion," said that gentleman, with a sigh of relief. He was not ambitious.

"All ready?"

The violins began playing a shivery sort of music and up the curtain went. The six attendant demons, led by the Wesleyan, who was in good voice now that he felt such a sense of relief, told the audience who they were and hailed their monarch in appropriate form. The Demon King, towering above them, dominating the scene superbly, replied in a voice of astonishing strength and richness. Then he sang the number allotted to him. It had nothing to do with Jack and Jill and very little to do with demons, being a rather commonplace bass song about sailors and shipwrecks and storms, with thunder and lightning effects supplied by the theatre. Undoubtedly this was the same song that had been rehearsed; the words were the same; the music was the same. Yet it all seemed different. It was really sinister. As you listened, you saw the great waves breaking over the doomed ships, and the pitiful little white faces disappearing in the dark flood. Somehow, the storm was much stormier. There was one great clap of thunder and flash of lightning that made all the attendant demons, the conductor of the orchestra, and a number of people in the wings, nearly jump out of their skins.

"And how the devil did you do that?" said the stage-manager, after running round to the other wing.

"That's what I said to 'Orace 'ere," said the man in charge of the two sheets of tin and the cannon ball.

"Didn't touch a thing that time, did we, mate?" said Horace.

"If you ask me, somebody let off a firework, one o' them big Chinese crackers, for that one," his mate continued. "Somebody monkeying about, that's what it is."

And now a white spotlight had found its way on to the stage, and there, shining in its pure ray, was Miss Dulcie Farrar, the Fairy Queen, who was busy waving a silver wand.

She was also busy controlling her emotions, for somehow she felt unaccountably nervous. Opening night is opening night, of course, but Miss Farrar had been playing Fairy Queens for the last ten years (and Principal Girls for the ten years before them), and there was nothing in this part to worry her. She rapidly came to the conclusion that it was Mr. Ireton's sudden reappearance, after she had made up her mind that he was not turning up, that had made her feel so shaky, and this caused her to feel rather resentful. Moreover, as an experienced Fairy Queen who had had trouble with demons before, she was convinced that he was about to take more than his share of the stage. Just because he had hit upon such a good make-up! And it *was* a good make-up, there could be no question about that. That greenish face, those glittering eyes— really, it was awful. Overdoing it, she called it. After all, a panto *was* a panto.

Miss Farrar, still waving her wand, moved a step or two nearer, and cried:

"I know your horrid plot, you evil thing,
    And I defy you, though you are the Demon King."

"What you?" he roared, contemptuously, pointing a long forefinger at her.

Miss Farrar should have replied: "Yes, I, the Queen of Fairyland," but for a minute she could not get out a word. As that horribly long forefinger shot out at her, she had felt a sudden sharp pain and had then found herself unable to move. She stood there, her wand held out at a ridiculous angle, motionless, silent, her mouth wide open. But her mind was active enough. "Is it a stroke?" it was asking, feverishly.

"Like Uncle Edgar had that time at Greenwich. Oo, it must be. Oo, whatever shall I do? Oo. Oo. Ooooo."

"Ho-ho-ho-ho-ho." The Demon King's sinister baying mirth resounded through the theatre.

"Ha-ha-ha-ha-ha." This was from the Wesleyan and his friends, and was a very poor chorus of laughs, dubious, almost apologetic. It suggested that the Wesleyan and his friends were out of their depth, the depth of respectable Bruddersfordian demons.

Their king now made a quick little gesture with one hand, and Miss Farrar found herself able to move and speak again. Indeed, the next second, she was not sure that she had ever been *unable* to speak and move. That horrible minute had vanished like a tiny bad dream. She defied him again, and this time nothing happened beyond an exchange of bad lines of lame verse. There were not many of these, however, for there was the duet to be fitted in, and the whole scene had to be played in as short a time as possible. The duet, in which the two supernaturals only defied one another all over again, was early Verdi by way of the local musical director.

After singing a few bars each, they had a rest while the musical director exercised his fourteen instrumentalists in a most imposing operatic passage. It was during this halt that Miss Farrar, who was now quite close to her fellow-duettist, whispered: "You're in great voice, to-night, Mr. Ireton. Wish I was. Too nervous. Don't know why, but I am. Wish I could get it out like you."

She received, as a reply, a flash of those glittering eyes (it really was an astonishing make-up) and a curious little signal with the long forefinger. There was no time for more, for now the voice part began again.

Nobody in the theatre was more surprised by what happened then than the Fairy Queen herself. She could not believe that the marvellously rich soprano voice that came pealing and soaring belonged to her. It was tremendous. Covent Garden would have acclaimed it. Never before, in all her twenty years of hard vocalism, had Miss Dulcie Farrar sung like that, though she had always felt that *somewhere* inside her there was a voice of that quality only waiting the proper signal to emerge and then astonish the world. Now, in some fantastic fashion, it had received that signal.

Not that the Fairy Queen overshadowed her supernatural colleague. There was no overshadowing *him*. He trolled in a diapason bass, and with a fine fury of gesture. The pair of them turned that stolen and botched duet into a work of art and significance. You could hear Heaven and Hell at battle in it. The curtain came down on a good rattle of applause. They are very fond of music in Bruddersford, but unfortunately the people who attend the first night of the pantomime are not the people who are most fond of music, otherwise there would have been a furore.

"Great stuff, that," said Mr. Tom Burt, who was on the spot. "Never mind, Jim. Let 'em take a curtain. Go on, you two, take the curtain." And when they had both bowed their acknowledgments, Miss Farrar excited and trembling, the Demon King cool and amused, almost contemptuous, Mr. Burt continued: "That would have stopped the show in some places, absolutely stopped the show. But the trouble here is, they won't applaud, won't get going easily."

"That's true, Mr. Burt," Miss Farrar observed. "They take a lot of warming up here. I wish they didn't. Don't you, Mr. Ireton?"

"Easy to warm them," said the tall crimson figure.

"Well, if anything could, that ought to have done," the lady remarked.

"That's so," said Mr. Burt, condescendingly. "You were great, Ireton. But they won't let themselves go."

"Yes, they will." The Demon King, who appeared to be taking his part very seriously, for he had not yet dropped into his ordinary tones, flicked his long fingers in the air, roughly in the direction of the auditorium, gave a short laugh, turned away, and then somehow completely vanished, though it was not difficult to do that in those crowded wings.

Half an hour later, Mr. Burt, his manager, and the stage-manager, all decided that something must have gone wrong with Bruddersford. Liquor must have been flowing like water in the town. That was the only explanation.

"Either they're all drunk or I am," cried the stage-manager.

"I've been giving 'em pantomimes here for five-and-twenty years," said Mr. Burt, "and I've never known it happen before."

"Well, nobody can say they're not enjoying it."

"Enjoying it! They're enjoying it too much. They're going daft. Honestly, I don't like it. It's too much of a good thing."

The stage-manager looked at his watch. "It's holding up the show, that's certain. God knows when we're going to get through at this rate. If they're going to behave like this every night, we'll have to cut an hour out of it."

"Listen to 'em now," said Mr. Burt. "And that's one of the oldest gags in the show. Listen to 'em. Nay, dash it, they must be all half seas over."

What had happened? Why—this: that the audience had suddenly decided to let itself go in a fashion never known in

Bruddersford before. The Bruddersfordians are notoriously difficult to please, not so much because their taste is so exquisite but rather because, having paid out money, they insist upon having their money's worth, and usually arrive at a place of entertainment in a gloomy and suspicious frame of mind. Really tough managers like to open a new show in Bruddersford, knowing very well that if it will go there, it will go anywhere. But for the last half-hour of this pantomime there had been more laughter and applause than the Theatre Royal had known for the past six months. Every entrance produced a storm of welcome. The smallest and stalest gags set the whole house screaming, roaring, and rocking. Every song was determinedly encored. If the people had been specially brought out of jail for the performance, they could not have been more easily pleased.

"Here," said Johnny Wingfield, as he made an exit as a Dame pursued by a cow, "this is frightening me. What's the matter with 'em? Is this a new way of giving the bird?"

"Don't ask me," said the Principal Boy. "I wasn't surprised they gave me such a nice welcome when I went on, because I've always been a favourite here, as Mr. Burt'll tell you, but the way they're carrying on now, making such a fuss over nothing, it's simply ridiculous. Slowing up the show, too."

After another quarter of an hour of this monstrous enthusiasm, this delirium, Mr. Burt could be heard grumbling to the Principal Girl, with whom he was standing in that close proximity which Principal Girls somehow invite. "I'll tell you what it is, Alice," Mr. Burt was saying. "If this goes on much longer, I'll make a speech from the stage, asking 'em to draw it mild. Never known 'em to behave like this. And it's a funny thing, I was only saying to somebody—now who was it I said that to?—anyhow, I was only saying to somebody that I wished this audience would let themselves go a bit more. Well, now I wish they wouldn't. And that's that."

There was a chuckle, not loud, but rich, and distinctly audible.

"Here," cried Mr. Burt. "Who's that? What's the joke?"

It was obviously nobody in their immediate vicinity. "It sounded like Kirk Ireton," said the Principal Girl, "judging by the voice." But Ireton was nowhere to be seen. Indeed, one or two people who had been looking for him, both in his dressing-room and behind, had not been able to find him. But he would not be on again for another hour, and nobody had time to discover whether Ireton was drinking again or not. The odd thing was, though, that the audience lost its wild enthusiasm just as suddenly as it had found it, and long before the interval it had turned itself into the familiar stolid Bruddersford crowd, grimly waiting for its money's worth. The pantomime went on its way exactly as rehearsed, until it came to the time when the demons had to put in another appearance.

Jack, having found the magic water and tumbled down the hill, had to wander into the mysterious cavern and there rest awhile. At least, he declared that he would rest, but being played by a large and shapely female, and probably having that restless feminine temperament, what he did do was to sing a popular song with immense gusto. At the end of that song, when Jack once more declared that he would rest, the Demon King had to make a sudden appearance through a trap-door. And it was reported from below, where a spring-board was in readiness, that no Demon King had arrived to be shot on to the stage.

"Now where—oh, where—the devil has Ireton got to?" moaned the stage-manager, sending people right and left, up and down, to find him.

The moment arrived, Jack spoke his and her cue, and the stage-manager was making frantic signals to her from the wings.

"Ouh-wer," screamed Jack, and produced the most realistic bit of business in the whole pantomime. For the stage directions read *Shows fright*, and Jack undoubtedly did show fright, as well he (or she) might, for no sooner was the cue spoken than there came a horrible green flash, followed by a crimson glare, and standing before her, having apparently arrived from nowhere, was the Demon King. Jack was now in the power of the Demon King and would remain in those evil clutches until rescued by Jill and the Fairy Queen. And it seemed as if the Principal Boy had suddenly developed a capacity for acting (of which nobody had ever suspected her before), or else that she was thoroughly frightened, for now she behaved like a large rabbit in tights. That unrehearsed appearance of the Demon King seemed to have upset her, and now and then she sent uneasy glances into the wings.

It had been decided, after a great deal of talk and drinks round, to introduce a rather novel dancing scene into this pantomime, in the form of a sort of infernal ballet. The Demon King, in order to show his power and to impress his captive, would command his subjects to dance—that is, after he himself had indulged in a little singing, assisted by his faithful six. They talk of that scene yet in Bruddersford. It was only witnessed in its full glory on this one night, but that was enough, for it passed into civic history, and local landlords were often called in to settle bets about it in the pubs. First, the Demon King sang his second number, assisted by the Wesleyan and his friends. He made a glorious job of it, and after a fumbled opening and a sudden glare from him, the Wesleyan six made a glorious job of it too. Then the Demon

King had to call for his dancing subjects, who were made up of the troupe of girls known as Tom Burt's Happy Yorkshire Lasses, daintily but demonishly tricked out in red and green. While the Happy Yorkshire Lasses pranced in the foreground, the six attendants were supposed to make a few rhythmical movements in the background, enough to suggest that, if they wanted to dance, they could dance, a suggestion that the stage-manager and the producer knew to be entirely false. The six, in fact, could not dance and would not try very hard, being not only wooden but also stubborn Bruddersford baritones.

But now, the Happy Yorkshire Lasses having tripped a measure, the Demon King sprang to his full height, which seemed to be about seven feet two inches, swept an arm along the Wesleyan six, and commanded them harshly to dance. And they did dance, they danced like men possessed. The King himself beat time for them, flashing an eye at the conductor now and again to quicken that gentleman's baton, and his faithful six, all with the most grotesque and puzzled expressions on their faces, cut the most amazing capers, bounding high into the air, tumbling over one another, flinging their arms and legs about in an ecstasy, and all in time to the music. The sweat shone on their faces; their eyes rolled forlornly; but still they did not stop, but went on in crazier and crazier fashion, like genuine demons at play.

"All dance!" roared the Demon King, cracking his long fingers like a whip, and it seemed as if something had inspired the fourteen cynical men in the orchestral pit, for they played like madmen grown tuneful, and on came the Happy Yorkshire Lasses again, to fling themselves into the wild sport, not as if they were doing something they had rehearsed a hundred times, but as if they, too, were inspired. They joined the orgy of the bounding six, and now, instead of there being only eighteen Happy Lasses in red and green, there seemed to be dozens and dozens of them. The very stage seemed to get bigger and bigger, to give space to all these whirling figures of demoniac revelry. And as they all went spinning, leaping, cavorting crazily, the audience, shaken at last out of its stolidity, cheered them on, and all was one wild insanity.

Yet when it was done, when the King cried, "Stop!" and all was over, it was as if it had never been, as if everybody had dreamed it, so that nobody was ready to swear that it had really happened. The Wesleyan and the other five all felt a certain faintness, but each was convinced that he had imagined all that wild activity while he was making a few sedate movements in the background. Nobody could be quite certain about anything. The pantomime went on its way; Jack was rescued by Jill and the Fairy Queen (who was now complaining of neuralgia); and the Demon King allowed himself to be foiled, after which he quietly disappeared again. They were looking for him when the whole thing was over except for that grand entry of all the characters at the very end. It was his business to march in with the Fairy Queen, the pair of them dividing between them all the applause for the supernaturals. Miss Farrar, feeling very miserable with her neuralgia, delayed her entrance for him, but as he was not to be found, she climbed the little ladder at the back alone, to march solemnly down the steps towards the audience. And the extraordinary thing was that when she was actually making her entrance, at the top of those steps, she discovered that she was not alone, that her fellow-supernatural was there too, and that he must have slipped away to freshen his make-up. He was more demonish than ever.

As they walked down between the files of Happy Yorkshire Lasses, now armed to the teeth with tinsel spears and shields, Miss Farrar whispered: "Wish I'd arranged for a bouquet. You never get anything here."

"You'd like some flowers?" said the fantastic figure at her elbow.

"Think I would! So would everybody else."

"Quite easy," he remarked, bowing slowly to the foot-lights. He took her hand and led her to one side, and it is a fact—as Miss Farrar will tell you, within half an hour of your making her acquaintance—that the moment their hands met, her neuralgia completely vanished. And now came the time for the bouquets. Miss Farrar knew what they would be; there would be one for the Principal Girl, bought by the management, and one for the Principal Boy, bought by herself.

"Oo, look!" cried the Second Boy. "My gosh!—Brudders-ford's gone mad."

The space between the orchestral pit and the front row of stalls had been turned into a hothouse. The conductor was so busy passing up bouquets that he was no longer visible. There were dozens of bouquets, and all of them beautiful. It was monstrous. Somebody must have spent a fortune on flowers. Up they came, while everybody cheered, and every woman with a part had at least two or three. Miss Farrar, pink and wide-eyed above a mass of orchids, turned to her colleague among the supernaturals, only to find that once again he had quietly disappeared. Down came the curtain for the last time, but everybody remained standing there, with arms filled with expensive flowers, chattering excitedly. Then suddenly somebody cried, "Oo!" and dropped her flowers, and others cried, "Oo!" and dropped *their* flowers, until at last everybody who had had a bouquet had dropped it and cried "Oo!"

"Hot," cried the Principal Girl, blowing on her fingers, "hot as anything, weren't they? Burnt me properly. That's a nice trick."

"Oo, look!" said the Second Boy, once more. "Look at 'em all. Withering away." And they were, every one of them, all shedding their colour and bloom, curling, writhing, withering away. . . .

"Message come through for you, sir, an hour since," said the doorkeeper to the manager, "only I couldn't get at yer. From the Leeds Infirmary, it is. Says Mr. Ireton was knocked down in Boar Lane by a car this afternoon, but he'll be all right to-morrow. Didn't know who he was at first, so couldn't let anybody know."

The manager stared at him, made a number of strange noises, then fled, signing various imaginary temperance pledges as he went.

"And another thing," said the stage-hand to the stage-manager. "That's where I saw the bloke last. He was there one minute and next minute he wasn't. And look at the place. All scorched."

"That's right," said his mate, "and what's more, just you take a whiff—that's all, just take a whiff. Oo's started using brimstone in this the-ater? Not me nor you neither. But I've a good idea who it is."

BIOGRAPHY

John Boynton Priestley was born in 1894 in the suburb of Manningham, Bradford. He left Belle Vue High School at the age of 16 to go into the wool business, working as a clerk for Helm & Co, while determined to become a full-time writer. His first newspaper columns were published, while he was a teenager, in the 'Bradford Pioneer' (the weekly journal of Bradford's Labour Party).

Once World War One broke out Priestley joined the West Riding Regiment and served throughout the war. He was wounded three times, served on the Western Front and in the Battle of Loos, and in 1917 he was commissioned as an officer before injuries sustained in a gas attack led him to be classified as unfit for active service. After the War, Priestley studied at Trinity Hall, Cambridge, and on leaving university his career as a professional writer began. His first book, 'Brief Diversions', appeared in 1922, by then he was publishing widely in the *Spectator*, *Times Literary Supplement* and a range of newspapers.

Priestley's third novel 'The Good Companions' was published in 1929 and within a few months became a publishing sensation, as well as being awarded the James Tait Black

Memorial Prize. His subsequent novel, 'Angel Pavement', cemented his position as a major writer and in the 1930s he began to write plays that would become staples of the West End theatre. Also in the 1930s Priestley would travel throughout England and his increasing interest in social problems would lead to one of his most lasting works, 'English Journey'.

During World War Two Priestley presented the BBC Radio programme *Postscript*, which drew audiences of up to 16 million and led Graham Greene to describe Priestley as "a leader second only in importance to Mr Churchill".

Priestley's most famous play 'An Inspector Calls' appeared in 1945, it is still produced all over the world. In November 1957 a Priestley article for the *New Statesman* attacked Aneurin Bevan's policy of abandoning unilateral nuclear disarmament, so many people wrote to the magazine supporting Priestley's views that Kingsley Martin, the editor of the *New Statesman*, organised a meeting where the Campaign for Nuclear Disarmament (CND) was formed.

In 1960 Priestley published 'Literature and Western Man', a major survey of Western literature from the fifteenth-century to his own time. In 1977 he accepted the Order of Merit.

J.B. Priestley died on August 14th 1984. After his death Michael Foot, a former leader of the Labour party, described Priestley as "the conscience of a nation" and Bradford City Council commissioned a statue of Priestley, which now stands outside the National Media Museum looking across Priestley's native city.

THE J.B. PRIESTLEY SOCIETY

The Society welcomes new members and anyone is welcome to join. It has an attractive membership package; a varied social calendar; and offers a wide range of in-house publications and other opportunities to learn more about and discuss Priestley.

The Society is a member of The Alliance of Literary Societies.

For further information about J.B. Priestley, Society activities and great benefits of membership visit our website at: *www.jbpriestley-society.com*